CALL
OF THE
SUN
CHILD

CALL
OF THE
SUN
CHILD

FRANCESCA G. VARELA

owl house books
AN IMPRINT OF HOMEBOUND PUBLICATIONS

PUBLISHED BY OWL HOUSE BOOKS
AN INPRINT OF HOMEBOUND PUBLICATIONS

For bulk ordering information or permissions write:
Homebound Publications, PO Box 1442
Pawcatuck, Connecticut 06379 United States of America

FIRST EDITION
ISBN: 978-1-938846-18-2 (PBK)

BOOK DESIGN
Front Cover Image: © Tithi Luadthong | Shutterstock.com
Cover and Interior Design: Leslie M. Browning

Library of Congress Cataloging-in-Publication Data

Varela, Francesca G.
  Call of the sun child / by Francesca G. Varela. — First edition.
    pages cm
  ISBN 978-1-938846-18-2 (pbk.)
  I. Title.
  PZ7.V4266Cal 2014
  [Fic]—dc23

2013049161

10 9 8 7 6 5 4 3 2

Dedicated to Misty

CHAPTER ONE

He turns and looks at me with gray slanted eyes, reaching out one hand. *Let me help you.* I hear the words before his mouth moves. They plead, they echo off his pink, outstretched palm. His features are blurry. Behind this man is a light that hisses and spits with great tenderness. It grows brighter. I think I'll never see again. Then the light swallows the man.

I tell Mom about the dream the next night. She takes a pert sip of water, gulps back her Vitamin D pill. There's a clang as she sets her glass down on the metal kitchen table. We've just woken up and this act is too loud for the empty apartment.

Now the refrigerator seems to hum louder, the newscaster on the TV wall is screaming wildly, the antique clock ticks relentlessly down the hall. All sound is bounced out of place and stretched into every quiet corner. I swallow my own pill, carefully avoiding the cold brush of metal against my bare elbows.

"Sounds almost like the sun," Mom tries to smile at me, then seems to remember how tired she is. They haven't even turned the light on yet. She pours us some cereal. "I think we're almost out of milk tablets."

"How do you know what the sun looks like?" I eye the TV wall warily.

A blonde haired reporter is interviewing Kern Bradley, the opponent running for president of our facility. They sit stiffly beneath white walls and stainless steel. Kern clears his throat roughly, nodding his head. Everyone knows he won't win. He wants to allow in new outsiders.

"I've seen it in old movies. They used to show us in school. Don't they do that anymore?"

"No. They don't. I guess they don't want us to know what we're missing out on."

"Please, don't start with that again. Just remember how lucky we are to live here. Would you rather be on the outside and have to fend for yourself? There's nothing left out there." She turns to me, her spoon halfway to her beige lips.

"I know, I know. Sorry."

We eat staring at the wall. I avoid looking at the empty third chair. Mom puts her bowl in the dishwasher just as the light is turned on. At first it's a muted red glow that drips through the window. They turn the light on gradually for comfort, so it feels natural. At least, that's what they tell us. Who knows what a sunrise is really like.

The dense, silver ceiling encircling us has always been closed. Solar panels on the facility's roof bring us the sun's power. Water comes from a distant sea before the salt is taken out. Food and clothing are made in an industrial facility, then shipped here on the underground trains. No one goes to the outside, and no one enters the sloping walls of the Circadia Stable Living Facility. Our home. Our world, really.

I've always wanted to go to the perimeter. There are rumors that there used to be a secret window where you could watch the outside world. It was only a crack in the wall, a flaw in the government's design. An old man supposedly covered up this hole with a worn gray cloth. He only let certain people look through it, and the brave would reach their hands out to caress the moving air.

The government could never track down the window. Some say

the old man died of skin cancer from the radiation that leaked in during the day. Others swear that one night an outsider came and stabbed him through the hole with a knife. All agree that he's gone.

It's brighter now. Yellow light falls down from the domed ceiling. I hurry to the bathroom, splash my face with water and brush my teeth. Sometimes I wonder what I'd look like if I painted my face like the ancients did. Would I be prettier with rings of black around my brown eyes, with red dust on my cheeks? No, I'd just get weird looks, walking around like a photo from our history text.

Mom's already dressed in her white polyester work outfit. She touches the wall in the kitchen to turn off the TV. I shuffle past her into my room to change. We shove our phones in our pockets and leave.

"You see," Mom says as we go down the elevator, "if we lived on the outside we would have to have locks on our doors. There would be criminals walking around *everywhere*."

All the government has to do is claim that you're unfit for the facility. Then they open the steel, bolted door to the outside, the *only* door, and shove you out. The air purification systems are always buzzing on full blast for a few days after that happens. We don't have a jail. The government feels that banishment is a proper penalty for any offense.

"Yeah, I guess you're right."

A man and a woman are singing in the middle of the street. The woman sits on a plastic chair, towering over a small black bowl for money offerings. Her hair is bright red and shining. I can hear them before we're out of the lobby, wailing the wordless rhythms that are so popular right now. They lean in towards each other, the man closing his eyes passionately behind thick glasses.

Several people bend down and toss a few coins in the bowl. No one stops to listen. Clouds of white-clothed people rush down the concrete path, ghosts against the square gray buildings behind them. The tallest building is six stories tall. If you stand on the roof you can reach up and touch the screws that hold together the ceiling, and smell the burning heat of the lights.

Mom and I follow the crowd to the thin silver train that slices the facility in half. The smiling doorman waves us on as we show him the passes on our phones. It takes only two minutes to travel the thirty miles to the business district.

I study the other passengers. Their light brown faces are tilted to the floor, their delicate fingers wrapped carefully around the handles on the wall. They are cleaners, grocery dispensary owners, hair stylists, scientists, students like me. A man with clear eyes glances up at me, and I jump, remembering my dream.

The train glides quietly to its destination. Mom kisses me on the cheek before we walk in opposite directions; she goes to her job at a clothing dispensary, and I go to school.

There's only one school in the facility, which ranges from kindergarten to the fourteenth grade. Only the rich kids move on to the exclusive college down the street because only they can afford it. They're the ones who grow up to wear bright colors, who become the government. My friend Alden says that the government wants it that way so the upper class will always stay in power. He must be right. One of the only requirements to run for office, or to even work for the government, is to be a college graduate.

"Hey, Sempra," Alden says as I sit down beside him in the accelerated tenth grade classroom. He's very thin and his ears are slightly pointy. No one ever talks to him but me.

The teacher, Ms. Morgan, sits stoically at the head of the long rectangular table, wrapped in painstakingly white robes. She's one of those people who are employed by the government. I once overheard Ms. Morgan ordering the elderly custodian with a missing finger to clean the room twice a day, at break and after school. The sharp smell of disinfectant emanates from every classroom, but it's always strongest in ours.

We take out our phones and huddle in towards the table we share *for better communication ability*. My eyes dart to the little round window in the corner, overlooking the near-empty street below. I wonder what it would be like to not have to go to school.

"Let's resume the history lesson from our last class. Please bring up the text on your phones," Ms. Morgan's voice is high and crisp, but her square face is lined and chubby, sagging at the chin like melting ice.

I've had my black touch-screen cell phone since I was a little kid. Everyone has. We're issued the standard model on our sixth birthdays, and keep the phones for most of our lives. To lose or damage your phone is grievously frowned upon.

Natalia's purple, sparkle covered phone shines gloatingly from across the table. She's the daughter of the current president of the facility, Harmond Nielson. Only the wealthy update their cell phones. Natalia's smooth, caramel skin is framed by stringy black hair with purple streaks.

When we were kids she told me that her goal in life would entail following in her father's footsteps, becoming president, and making sure that I was thrown out her first day in office. I shrugged and ran off to play with Alden, but Natalia's lips never quivered from their straight, smug line.

In the hands dangling above the elbows leaning on the table are mostly standard model phones. Only Karen, Bret, Natalia, and Greg hold colors and higher memory and enhanced durability.

"Now, we talked about how the ancient races of man were assimilated over time by hundreds of years of interbreeding, resulting in the mixed form we are today. Prejudice has thus been eliminated."

We follow along with the e-books on our phones as she talks about the ancient times of waste and pollution; of the great change, of how they hastily tried to remedy their mistakes, of how it was too late; of the creation of the facilities, and the way the founders only allowed in the people who could pay, so only productive citizens would lead the way to the new world.

"It was dangerous," Ms. Morgan keeps repeating, "the way they used to live in the open, under the burning sun. Skin cancer became as common as a cold. With the depleted ozone layer and the sun growing stronger, the ultraviolet rays were just too damaging. That's when society became nocturnal."

She hollowly explains how climate change made the world a desert, how the rising oceans buried entire cities and islands, how immense storms ravaged the land. How famine and drought left millions of bodies decaying in the sun. How mass extinction forced life out of balance, and death became more common than life. Nothing we haven't heard before.

"They had to run for their shelters when the sun came up, closing their steel shutters. They started living in windowless huts. That's how the outsiders still live. Like animals, having to fear something bigger than them.

"The old countries and governments of the time lost hold of society. A few world leaders stepped in, the founders, and saved humanity from chaos. They were geniuses. They constructed the facilities; seven for living purposes and five for industrial purposes, along with the underground train network connecting them.

"Our founders managed to create a safe, stable, and sustainable living environment in the midst of desolation. Not only have we functioned flawlessly for one hundred and fifty years, but we have managed to thrive and achieve a remarkably high standard of living on the limited resources available."

I look over at Alden, who is staring ponderously at the wall as though it is all of eternity. He sighs, locking his sad black eyes with mine. Then we learn about calculus and persuasive essays and the periodic table of elements, all from the mouth of Ms. Morgan and the minds of our phones. When the final bell buzzes we upload our work to the teacher's server and leave.

"Sempra," Alden stops, tugging on my arm when we're halfway to the train, "have you ever read the book *The Call of the Wild*? By Jack London?"

"No. I don't think that's on our reading list."

"No, it's not. It's not even on the e-book store. But look," he pulls a small, old-fashioned bound book from his pocket.

"Where did you get this?" I look around to make sure no one's watching us. The street is deserted. "You know we're not supposed to have paper. That should be in a museum or something. It's probably banned. If the government found out—"

"I just… found it on the ground. It was sitting beside a trashcan on my street. I already read it."

"What's that on the cover?" I point to a picture of a furry four-legged animal with its long snout turned up in the air.

"That's a wolf. I think they're extinct now. The story's about how a dog—I think dogs are probably still around somewhere, on the outside—um, it's about a dog that goes to the north when it used to be frozen, and he returns to the wilderness and lives with the wolves. Because dogs used to be wolves before humans domesticated them thousands of years ago," he gestures excitedly at the book as he talks.

"The wilderness. With the sun."

I haven't read much fiction. In school we only read modern books. The protagonist always has a steady job and spends their money on things that don't use up resources, like a new hairstyle. We only talk about the time before the facilities for history.

"Can I borrow it?" I ask quietly.

"Yeah, but don't show it to anyone. They might take it away. And give it back to me by tomorrow," he hands me the tiny hardback novel.

I open it up and press my nose to the page. It smells musty. I run my finger over the stitches binding it, over the yellowing paper. This came from trees, I tell myself. This came from the outside and from long ago.

"I'll take good care of it," I promise as we drift slowly towards the train.

CHAPTER TWO

*S*ometimes he pursued the call into the forest, looking for it as though it were a tangible thing, barking softly or defiantly, as the mood might dictate. He would thrust his nose into the cool wood moss, or into the black soil where long grasses grew, and snort with joy at the fat earth smells...

For the second time this year it rains. You can vaguely hear the gaunt drops of water slide down the domed roof. The drumming is offbeat, it longs for something green to perch on.

I imagine myself standing at the edge of a great canyon, with no roof, facing a wide horizon where tall grasses mimic the wind. And it would be raining, so I could feel what the earth feels and soak it up. Maybe I would stretch my arms out.

But— no. I shouldn't be thinking these things. It's the book. It makes me wish that I could go back in time. Like Mom says, we're lucky to live in the facility. Because it's safe here.

Maybe the rain is a sign. The first time I read a real book, about the outside, it rains. But what is the sign *for*?

Keeping one eye on my bedroom door as I read, I come close to the end of the book. Mom will be home from work soon. If anyone finds out about this, we'll be persecuted, and so will Alden. We should have reported it, like good citizens.

Once I give the book back to Alden I know he's going to hide it, treasure it. And even if we do turn it in, it's too late. The ideas are already in our heads forever.

It feels weird to turn the pages. I'm used to reading off of the tiny screen of my phone. Maybe I shouldn't, but I like this better. Probably just because it's forbidden. It's an *improper use of resources,* according to the government. I don't think they would want us reading *The Call of the Wild* anyway, even as an e-book. It would make everyone think too much. Alden says the government wants to be the only one who thinks. They want us citizens to be easily controlled.

I hear the thump of the front door and throw the book under my bed. I've never hidden anything from her before.

"Hi Mom," I walk into the living room.

"Hi, Sempra. How was school?" She has dark circles under her eyes. Her skin is like clay with pieces cut out. Work makes her tired.

Mom is one step away from working for the government. She's the saleslady for a clothing dispensary that the government owns. The government controls the factories that supply the clothes, and they pay the manager of the dispensary to run it. Then the manager pays my mom's salary with some of that money. It's the government that gets the profit from the clothes to use for factory maintenance. All dispensaries work the same way.

"It was good."

"Good. I'll start dinner."

We talk about the rain as she heats up frozen squares in the microwave. Our food looks like mush but is flavored like fruit and vegetables and bread. I don't know what it's made out of. But they add vitamins to it, so it's probably just like eating the real thing.

I really want to go back to my room and finish the last few pages. But first I must eat dinner, watch the news, and pretend that nothing extraordinary has happened.

The rain beats down harder than I've ever heard it. Finally I escape to the feral northland, to scurrying creatures in ancient forests that I'll never see. In my mind I can see the sky, but I can't imagine how it would feel to stand under something so vast.

When the long winter nights come on and the wolves follow their meat into the lower valleys, he may be seen running at the head of the pack through the pale moonlight or glimmering borealis, leaping gigantic above his fellows, his great throat a-bellow as he sings a song of the younger world, which is the song of the pack.

With my eyes shut I close the book. I don't understand all the words, but the pictures come clearly to my mind. Sinking into my pastel blue sheets, I fall asleep with it on my chest. Soft, dim lights beyond my window replace the brighter ones of earlier.

My mom opens the door a crack, peeking in to see if I'm awake. Her eyes fly to the picture of the wolf rising up and down with my waves of breathing. She stomps over and rips it out of my lifeless fingers.

"What the hell is this?" Mom says as though I were never even sleeping.

"Huh?" I mumble, half-asleep, thinking it's time to get up for school already. Then I see what she's holding. "Wait, no, Mom!"

I jump up and desperately try to grab it from her. She holds the book above her head so I can't reach it. For a moment I think she's evil, the way her red eyes are wide with fury, the way the tinted shadows calmly envelop her.

"Where did you get this? Do you have any idea what will happen if the government finds out?" She's yelling now, frantic.

"I—uh…"

"They don't want us reading unapproved books, they don't want us having paper. And we do what they say because otherwise they will *kick us out*. Is that what you want? It's not like there's any food dispensaries out there. We would starve. We would be homeless. It's not like the old stories, Sempra, I'm sorry but it's not. We would *die* on the outside. Is that what you want? Do you want to die? Your father…" Mom looks down at the tile floor, takes a deep breath. "You know what, I'm just going to destroy it and we'll forget it ever—"

"No, you can't! It's… it's not mine."

"Well whose is it, then?"

"Alden's." I immediately want to take it back.

"That scrawny little boy? Maybe you shouldn't spend so much time with him. If he gets into trouble and you're associated with him… we don't want to get into that."

"No, it's okay, Mom. I'll just give the book back to him tomorrow. He found it and I was curious and I asked if I could borrow it. That's all."

"All I want is to keep you safe, Sempra. That's all your father and I ever wanted. But sometimes I worry about you. You need to learn some common sense, how to behave in the real world," she brings the book out from behind her back and reluctantly places it in my hands.

Her mouth opens like she wants to say something else. Instead she walks out of the room.

"Sorry," I tell the last flick of her dark brown hair.

Her words press down on me like little flies. The book is tainted now, it's not fun anymore. I throw it back under my bed. This is a time when my father's absence makes everything empty. I don't remember him, but I imagine him to be just like me. He would take my side, hug me, tell me that it's okay to wonder. Wouldn't he?

The thin, square photo screen on my wall flashes through a slideshow of digital photos. One is a picture of him. He's holding me as a chubby blob of a baby, grinning under his unruly moustache. It was before he got sick. Mom says he was always reading, that he was smarter than anyone she knew. He worked at a food dispensary, too poor to be a scientist.

Soon I enter the velvety black world of sleep without dreams. Alden says that we dream every time we sleep, we just don't always remember them. Some stories of our unconscious are lost before we wake up.

I remember hearing once of a little girl who sleep-walked every day. She was pulled without seeing, her rumpled yellow hair flying behind her, and wouldn't stop until she reached the door to the outside. People made faces. They frowned and looked away. The tall door guards knew her by name, and always walked the little girl home. Her ashamed parents took her to sleep specialists. Eventually she grew out of it, returning less and less often. She went on to work for the government.

What was she chasing, everyone asks? But I know the answer. And so do they.

That night we have breakfast in silence again. On the train I avoid everyone's gaze, worrying that they can read my guilt and sense the book bulging in my pocket. There is no kiss goodbye when Mom and I part ways.

"Do you have it?" Alden scoots his chair toward mine.

"I'll give it back to you after school," I pat my left pocket that holds both this and my phone.

"What did you think of it?"

"Maybe we shouldn't talk about that here," I whisper, my hands folded in my lap.

"Oh come on, no one's going to know what we're talking about."

I want to tell him about what happened. But then he might be mad at me for being so careless. He might feel betrayed that I told my mom that I got it from him.

"How do you know they don't have . . . hidden microphones in here?"

"Fine, we'll wait until after school."

School unfolds in front of me but I can't focus. I consider expelling all wild ideas from my head. Maybe it would be easier to just listen to my mom. But how can I, when I keep hearing wolves sing to a moon and seeing those gray eyes dance listlessly in circles?

"I think the book could be applied to man just as much as wolves," I say daringly when we're out of the building and away from all things living.

"That's exactly what I thought. If humans went back to the wild, could they live like our ancestors did? Could they survive?"

"Probably not. It's been too long."

"But physically we haven't changed all that much. I bet we could do it."

"Maybe we haven't changed, but the environment has."

"I guess. We'd have to adapt. The outsiders live out there. Don't you wonder what it's like? Do you think there's still snow somewhere, and dog sleds, and the aurora borealis?"

"I can't stop wondering things like that," I look up at the ceiling, "but I don't think we'll ever know."

"If the Earth is dead like they try to make us believe, maybe parts of it are still alive. The government doesn't want us to know anything. They keep us trapped in here like their little pets."

"We're not trapped." I sound like my mom.

"I know. But you know what I mean. They know that we don't have any other options, and they take advantage of it. I don't know. Maybe there is no outside world. This could be it. This could be the whole world. Maybe they've lied to us about everything."

He sounds like a crazed revolutionary. *The Call of the Wild* has had even more of an effect on him than it did on me.

"You're crazy…"

Alden grows quiet. I can tell he's been letting these thoughts cultivate in his mind for a long time. This is their manifestation. His face shows a discontent scowl as he retraces his words, our conversation. I slide the book out.

"Thanks for letting me borrow it."

"Sure . . . Sempra?"

"Yeah?"

"I wonder who put it there," he looks down at the cover.

"Me too, Alden. Me too."

"See you tomorrow."

Now I feel bad for not saying more. I should've let him know that the same rebellious ideas have pulsed through my own thoughts. Why did I try to act superior, *normal*, when I'm not? I shake my head as I make my way back to the apartment.

How can we both feel this way? It must be our instincts. They're telling us that this isn't right, this lifestyle isn't natural. We are the domesticated version of our ancestors. We are dogs who used to be wolves.

CHAPTER THREE

The temperature in the facility is always seventy degrees. This, they say, is the perfect comfort zone between sweating and having to wear a sweater. But tonight there is something wrong. Something's broken. I wish I had a jacket, but that would be a waste of resources.

All that is gray seems to be captured by icy blue. It must be at least fifty degrees. The stiff air, pushed around by the conditioning and ventilation systems, is sharp. And still we must go to school. Still we must venture out into unknown discomfort. There is no reminder of the powerful sun we cower from. He's busy, after all, burning the other side of the world right now.

The chill is a thousand needles breaking through my thin white tunic. I'm almost to school. But there won't be any heat there, either. All buildings are hooked up to the central system.

"There has been a mechanical error in the heating department," said the blonde man on the news before I left. "The government would like to assure everyone that the problem is being addressed, and that the temperature will be back to normal in about thirty minutes. Please excuse the inconvenience."

Mom says that this happened once when she was a little girl. Every twenty years or so parts gets worn out and they have to replace them.

"So they're *not* perfect," Alden raises his eyebrows. His bare arms are sprinkled with goose bumps.

"Why didn't you wear a long sleeve shirt? It's freezing."

"I don't have any."

Ms. Morgan doesn't even acknowledge that anything is abnormal, although she looks nice and warm in her double layer of robes. We begin class, but are soon interrupted when a tall boy walks in.

"Yes, yes. What do you want?" Ms. Morgan asks the boy with shaggy brown hair that's highlighted green.

"Is this the accelerated tenth grade class?" His voice is strong but his eyes look unsure.

"Yes it is . . . Are you Timothy?"

"That's me," he folds his hands behind his back.

"Class, Timothy here has been moved up from the standard," she spits it like they are far beneath her, the way she talks about the outsiders, "tenth grade class. Timothy, you can go have a seat. I'll send you the class list of phone numbers. Now, we were just talking about governmental order."

He takes the empty chair next to mine. I think about saying something but don't want to disrupt class. Instead I offer him a smile. When he grins back I realize how very good looking he is. I glance from the corner of my eye at his strong jaw, his angular face. My breathing grows shallow. I'm not cold anymore. He smells like soap, like fresh minty soap.

Then he lays his phone down on the table. I let out my breath. Bright blue with green stripes. He's rich, he's handsome, and he's above me in status. I know he sees my plain phone, but he doesn't seem repulsed. He doesn't shove his way across the table to join the other wealthy ones.

The only way to become rich if you're not born that way is to marry up. It's been done, but not often. There is only one rule concerning love; no more than one child per partner is allowed. Overpopulation is a threat that never ceases. If your family gets too big you'll be thrown out into the dust, newborn baby and all.

Twins or other multiples are the only exception. *They* have siblings to grow up with, since their parents didn't have a choice. Some people also have half or step siblings if their parents were divorced and remarried.

Alden is either bored or angry. He's clenching his phone like he wants to kill it, and won't look away from its screen. In my peripheral vision I see Timothy turn his head in my direction. I bite my lip. Was that aimed at me, or Ms. Morgan?

As school ends I stand up very slowly, hoping he'll say something to me.

"Come on Sempra, what are you waiting for?" Alden yells impatiently from the door.

"Sempra. I like your name. I'm Timothy," he's standing next to me, towering over the top of my head.

"Thanks. Nice to meet you," I shake his warm hand, hoping mine isn't sweaty.

"You too," he starts toward the door.

"Bye."

The temperature is normal again. It feels good not to have to clench my teeth or cross my arms. Alden is quiet as we fulfill our daily walk together to the train. I expect him to say something. About the cold, about the book, about Timothy. Anything.

"So if it was that cold *inside* the facility, imagine how cold it must get on the *outside* at night," I try to get him talking. When he just nods, features limp, I go on. "Come on, what's wrong?"

"Nothing."

"Is it Timothy?"

"No."

"Why don't you like him?"

"There's just . . . something about him that I don't trust."

"What, just because he's rich? I liked him."

"Yeah," he snorts. "I could tell."

"What if I married him. Then *I'd* be rich."

"So?"

"Well, would you still trust me?"

"It would depend on whether you went to college or not. That's where they all get brainwashed."

I smile. He's back.

Alden and I found each other on testing day. It was the first day of kindergarten. We were huddled in the corner of a sterile classroom with the other shy children. Our parents had walked us in, nudging us to a little row of chairs. They left us feeling restless as we blinked back hot tears.

A little boy with dark circles under his eyes sat on his knees, lip quivering. As the teachers called us over to determine whether we'd be placed in the accelerated program, he clasped his hands over his ears.

The other kids fidgeted with their hair. They whined for their parents. I curiously tapped Alden on the shoulder and asked what he was doing. Trying to disappear, he mumbled. I sat down cross-legged beside him, concentrating on growing wings and flying home. The teachers found us, grabbed our hands and led us to our tests.

We've clung to each other over the years. We're different than the other kids. If it wasn't for Alden, I might be normal. He's always been the more extreme, the less accepted. On occasion our classmates will chat with me, but not Alden. They know his parents are cleaners, only one step above factory workers, and they know he is skinny and odd. This is enough for them. There's no need to look at him.

My phone buzzes. I gasp.

"It's Timothy."

"Great," Alden saunters away with his hands in his pockets, leaving me standing alone in the middle of the street.

Timothy's text asks if I want to see "The No-Children Club" at the movie theater. I've already seen it, and hated it, but my fingers quickly type out yes.

He's waiting for me in front of the brown, one-story theater in the entertainment district. I wave to him; he's leaning against the wall, arms crossed over his chest. Muted previews play on the wall beside the ticket booth. Flashing red and yellow lights pull savagely on the narrow walls around us. The rows of buildings feel heavy on top, like they'll fall over. Then we would be crushed beneath piles of heaviness. We wouldn't be able to breathe.

This is the street where everyone comes to spend their money on plays, concerts, shows. At this time of night most of the adults are still at work. There are only a few students, laughing in front of steel doorways. Their laughter sounds like concrete being poured. It's false, gushing out of their mouths in fat, dripping chunks. It's . . . yes, it's bitter. Like someone placed them there. I want them to leave.

But then it might be too quiet. Sometimes it scares me, how the silence moves. It feels like you can hear the other side of the facility, up and over everything. I feel this same emptiness when Mom has gone to sleep and I stare awake at the window. Alone with each breath.

Timothy hands me a ticket, then holds the door open for me. We don't say much until we're sitting down in the dark theater. It smells slightly musty. The screen is enormous, the full height of the building. Facing it are long barricades of plush benches with back-rests. There is one other couple in the back of the room.

"I'm glad you could come," he says, squinting. He looks much older all of a sudden. With a jolt I wonder if this is the same boy from school. Then I feel silly.

"Me too. This was a good idea." I pretend to watch the previews. "So, how did you like your first class with Ms. Morgan?"

"She's..." he laughs, "she's interesting. You know, I bet she has some deep dark secret that she's never told anyone. Doesn't she seem like the type?"

I'm surprised that he would say something so Alden-like, so odd.

"Yeah, you're right. What kind of secret could she have? Maybe it's murder. Maybe she bored a student to death."

"I could believe that." He looks over at me, arms draped over the backrest. "And you, Miss Sempra? What kind of secrets do you have?"

I blink a few times, lick my lips. Timothy's long, straight nose holds my gaze.

"That," I whisper, "is something I'll never tell."

We don't say anything else for the rest of the movie. Neither of us laugh when the actresses make a pact never to have children. Neither of us crack a smile when, in the end, they can't resist temptation and each have one perfect baby. Sullenly, our eyes mop the screen.

"We should've just hung out," I say when we're out on the crowded street, "that was a horrible movie."

"I don't know, I thought it was a pretty good first date," he smiles shyly with his lips closed, thick eyebrows raised.

"Date, huh?"

"If that's okay with you."

"Of course."

Timothy suddenly tears his phone out from his white pant pocket. I remember now that he's rich. His nostrils flare as he reads the screen.

"Oh, uh, sorry," he nervously jiggles his blue cell phone, and takes a step back, "I have to take this. But see you tomorrow, okay?"

"Oh, okay . . . Bye..." I want to reach out for him and give him a hug. But he's already gone.

The light is pale and my stomach growls. Despite the suddenness of his departure, I feel thunderously happy. Timothy. Timothy makes me happy.

CHAPTER FOUR

"So . . . does anyone ever call you Tim?" Alden tilts his head up to match his voice.

"Um, no," Timothy scratches his chin, laughing as though this is the most absurd question he has ever heard. "Does anyone call you Al?"

Alden's chair squeaks against the tile floor as he leans back. He crosses then uncrosses his slender arms. Ms. Morgan is clasping her hands together in the front of the room, ready to start class.

Across the table, Natalia glares at the empty sliver of air between me and Timothy. When he walked in a few minutes ago, calm and handsome, she had motioned him over.

"Why don't you sit over here with us? We're..." she had patted her sparkling phone, "more your type. Don't you think?"

Timothy bent down to her level, leaning on his knees. He looked down at the floor then into her eyes. Natalia sat stiffly, back straight. Her face reminded me of thin glass. She had thrust her hands up. "Well?" her gesture said. The room was silent.

"Thanks for the offer, but I think I would rather sit with Sempra."

Simple, honest, straightforward. Natalia breathed in sharply. She ran a finger over her sparse eyebrow and wrinkled her forehead. I welcomed Timothy to my left side.

I see a sadness in Natalia. It comes, not from anger or embarrassment, but from fear. She sighs. Her shoulders slump forward like the ground is a magnet. It's only in these pockets of time that Natalia stops resisting the pull.

With dry dignity she flicks a strand of hair out of her face. Then she sits up, crosses her ankles. She's trying so hard to be good enough, so hard that she never will be until the moment she stops trying.

Maybe she's overwhelmed, being the president's daughter. But it's far worse to be the daughter of a dead man. I have no true memories of him. Nothing. Only pictures and stories and what my mind has drawn.

Sometimes I pretend that he has just gone away. My daddy is off on a trip, that's all. He'll be back someday. Then he will tell me stories in his deep, smooth voice. Then we will sit together, and watch movies. Then he will smooth back my hair and kiss me good morning on the cheek.

It's hard to admit that I'll never be able to hug him, to bury my nose into his chest next to his armpit. I will never hear him say, *I love you, Sempra.*

Did he have the chance to genuinely love me? It was the idea of me. That's what he loved. He knew me for a month. I never knew him. I never will. So how can *I say* I love him? How can I not?

No one knows for sure what the government does with dead bodies. Some say that they're thrown out the door. I've heard that they're heaped in a festering pile on the outside, a few feet from the facility. Their dead brown eyes stare into the sun. Wind rustles through their brittle, moaning eyelashes. They decompose, melt to the ground, and rejoin the earth they never truly touched.

That is, if the outsiders don't get to them first.

Okay, the government probably just cremates the corpses. But I still hope their ashes are taken to the outside. I'd like to think of my father returning to the earth, his basic elements nourishing life. Or he could be a tree somewhere. That's what happens when you die. You get to become wild again. And his spirit...maybe that's in a tree too. In leaves that drink sun and spiraling roots that sing to dirt.

"I'm going to skip school tomorrow," Timothy says smugly after class. The bright lights magnify his features. When he turns his head I can make out the fuzzy outline of a pale moustache.

"Well, it was nice knowing you then," Alden draws out the last word, the corner of his wide mouth twitching with a suppressed smile.

"You have to go to school," I itch my arm, "or else—"

"Or else I'll be exiled to the outside? You're allowed to stay home if you're sick. I'll just text them and pretend to be my dad."

I don't know what to say. Oh Timothy. Not only is he good-looking and unique, he's a risk taker. He's the kind who will grab your hand and lead you on an adventure. I envision us becoming a wild and independent couple, daring to do what we please and never getting caught. We would watch old movies of the sun. Flipping our hair around, we would run through the streets and scream.

He wants me to skip with him or he wouldn't have told us. Could we do it? Could we fool society? Is this taste of freewill worth the consequences? Both of us sick on the same night might be too obvious. I've never heard of anyone skipping school.

And Alden, Alden who always wants to fight the government. What does he think? My mom would be furious, that's certain. But Alden . . .

"So you're going to hide inside all night?" Alden shakes his head. "If anyone sees you you'll get reported."

"Yeah," Timothy shrugs.

"I'm in," I say.

Timothy nods to Alden, gives me a side hug, then disappears. He doesn't ride home with us. We sway with the train, holding on to the rough looped handles. Alden is quiet again. Quiet sewn to quiet on the empty train. I breathe in what smells like glue and plastic.

"You don't want me to skip school, do you." I don't look back at him.

"No, not really," his voice is one step away from monotone. "You're just going to get in trouble."

"But I thought you would like the idea of defying authority."

"Not for this. Not for nothing. I just . . . want to know the truth about . . . about the world. I want to know the way things really are. You don't break the law just to break the law. You do it because it means something."

But I still want to spend a night away from school. We get the last day of each month off. So do most jobs. That's it. Perpetual brainwashing, Alden says. Whatever perpetual means.

I want to sleep in, and not have to sit in a stiff chair for hours. It would be my secret stand against the over-controlling government. A night to think for myself. Doesn't that mean something?

By dinner I'm a little nervous. Should I go through with it? Mom smiles sleepily from across the table. Then she sneezes loudly into her shoulder. With a start I realize that I'll need to send the text from her phone. Otherwise the school will know it's me. I'll just have to wake up before Mom, sneak into her room, and return the phone before she knows what happened. Yes. That will work.

I can't sleep. When will it be late enough to text the school? When's the soonest I can do it? I imagine lounging on the couch after Mom has gone to work, texting Timothy about our plans . . .

Wait. Mom will notice if I don't leave for school. We ride the train together. She'll know. I could just get back on the train and come home after we part ways. But then the train people will see me. They might figure it out. They might turn me in.

Or maybe I could even tell *Mom* that I'm sick, and she'll text the school for me. Yeah, that could work. I close my eyes.

Bitter coughing wakes me up. I wander into the living room and see Mom huddled under a white blanket on the couch. She looks pale, her nose blotchy red, and her hair is flying in crazy tufts.

"Hi, honey," her voice is scratchy and unsteady, "I don't feel good. I think I'll stay home from work today."

Mom turns back to the TV wall. She's watching a rerun of the presidential debate between Kern Bradley and Harmond Nielson, Natalia's father. President Nielson's dark eyes casually dart down to the script he's reading from. Bradley, with his long wavy hair pulled back in a respectful ponytail, pounds his fist toward the elusive sky. A cheer erupts from the audience. The president's heavy face scowls.

I text Timothy that I'm going to school. If Mom is home all night, what's the point of skipping? I would just have to fake sick the whole time.

Alden's glad when I come to school. He scoots his chair over to make room for me, smiling shyly inward. I watch his plain gray shoes swinging back and forth under the table. He doesn't say anything. I'm sure he's thinking that I made the right choice. Maybe . . . maybe I won't tell him that I wasn't the one who made it.

Timothy never replies to my text. Is he mad? Or still sleeping? He'll probably sit at home and watch TV for hours. Just like my mom. Maybe it wouldn't have been that much fun to skip.

"What happened to Timothy? Did he need a day off from giving to the *poor*?" Natalia rolls her eyes at us.

We know we're not the elite. There's nothing we can do about it. Alden says that these static classes are designed to make us feel inferior. That way we're easier to control. It's all about control, he says. Power and control.

"Natalia, I heard that your father is going to lose the re-election," Greg, the quietest of the rich kids, grins at us. His teeth used to be crooked and stained, but now they glow white against his olive skin.

"Oh really? I know for a fact that he is going to win, *Buck*," Natalia wrinkles her nose, shakes her head. This was Greg's old nickname. Back then his crusty buckteeth hung low and wide above his chin.

Alden gives me a look. Buck. That's the name of the protagonist in our great secret, in *The Call of the Wild*. I lean against my warm hand and let out a deep breath. No. They don't know anything. How could they?

But really . . . really I want them to know. I want them to feel my defiance. To quiver beneath my worldliness. Look up at me, I will say. Look up at me even though I'm shorter than you.

Can I become this person? They are the ones with the eyes. If I am me to myself, who am I to them? It's not acceptance that I want. It's too late for that. I want respect.

What will my future be? The square shelves of a dispensary job. A quiet, balding husband who agrees too easily. And one child. One boy or girl who will shove the cycle onward. Maybe Alden was right about being trapped.

I need to know if there's more. If there's something we're missing. And what life is for . . . these blank walls of life . . .

The yellow light paints Ms. Morgan's colorless hair. She shows her teeth. It's not a smile. I don't think she's ever smiled in her life. Her bright pink gums are almost orange. They're like a dirty wrinkled cloth that's soaked and torn. What does Ms. Morgan do when she gets home? Is there someone who pats her vein-stroked hand? Who sits beside her? Did she once have a mother? Who created this . . . this stoic beast?

Ms. Morgan once ran for president of the facility. It was very long ago, right after she graduated from college. She lost, of course, or else she wouldn't be here now. This was what ruined her life, I suppose. One traumatic moment of disappointment. Which led to doubt, and, in turn, bitterness. I have to admit that I'm very glad she didn't win.

"Complete math problems one to seventy-five odd, and read chapters two and three of A Citizen's Guide to Society. And don't forget about the test on Friday," our teacher reads off of her phone just before the bell sounds.

Suddenly a vague distaste in my stomach burns into anger. I glower at the naive, chatting voices of my classmates. Maybe I should've skipped class anyway. I could have told Mom that I was going to school and then met up with Timothy instead. But then I would have had to text the school from her phone somehow . . . Oh, how can they be happy when our lives are so stiff?

They don't know anything. And neither do I. But at least I question. Me and Alden and Timothy. We're the only ones.

"You know, why would you even want to be rich? We all live in the same size of apartments. We all eat the same food. All they get are better phones and different clothes. And maybe they can see more movies. So what? What's so great about being rich?" I draw my thoughts out of my head and into Alden's sharp, angled ears.

Our feet walk us to the train, the familiar path memorized after years of repetition. Always we are slower than the other kids. We slide our shoes like snakes against the dull pavement. The air tastes just like it did in the school. Stale.

If this air were a color, it would be reddish brown. It never changes. Buildings share their breath in and out. Rows and rows of structures and corners keep us ambling in straight lines.

"The only good thing about being rich is freedom," a voice comes from behind us.

I whip my head around to see Timothy walking toward us with his arms outstretched. He rests his long, muscular limbs on our shoulders, sandwiched between me and Alden.

"What are you doing here? I thought you were skipping school," Alden grumbles. He tilts his neck and slides out from under Timothy's armpit.

"I already did. I thought I'd come meet you," Timothy stares down his arm and into my eyes. "I was getting bored."

"What if someone saw you? They'll know you weren't really sick." I feel the heat from his heavy arm jump through my shirt. He doesn't smell like mint anymore. No, he doesn't smell like anything.

"I just made a quick recovery, that's all. Hey, you wanna go for a walk?" He moves away from me to check his cell phone.

"A walk?" I wait for an explanation.

"Yeah."

"You mean . . . you want to . . . just . . . walk around?"

"Yeah . . . you never do that?"

"Oh, well, uh, sometimes, I guess. From the train to my apartment."

"But never just for fun?"

"No," I laugh, "is that a fun thing to do?"

"I think so. Let me show you," Timothy holds out his hand.

My dream flashes from a million miles away. The man with those odd eyes . . . *Let me help you* . . . But Timothy isn't him. Timothy doesn't have the same feeling. Or the same eyes.

Alden keeps going to the train. I don't say anything because Timothy doesn't either. My chest feels empty. For a second I want to yell goodbye, even invite him along. There goes my best friend. Lonely and alone.

But here I go, off with a good-looking guy who actually thinks. I grab Timothy's waiting hand.

We talk about aliens. And rocks. And rain. Timothy manages to give his opinions without being offensive. He doesn't force it on you. I try to be the same way, to be graceful.

No one thinks much of us as we pass through the outskirts of the living district. They think we're walking home. But they don't see us continue on, each story connected to make it last.

This isn't the way we're taught to have fun. And still it is. Timothy was right.

"Where are we going?" I finally ask.

"Wherever we end up."

CHAPTER FIVE

They're exiling a middle-aged man. *He's a criminal,* the people hiss, *thank goodness they finally caught him.* Do they even know what he did?

Crowded streets cheer. I can smell their great pools of sweat. I can hear them yell. Oh, how sound carries when it's lifted by hatred.

The news shows two guards marching him to the door. His dark hands shake beneath bright steel handcuffs. The poor, nameless man. He watches the ground the whole time. A prim beard streaked with gray coats his fragile chin. Clean white suit, worn black shoes, wire-framed glasses. That's all they let him take.

And what did he do? He lost his job. No money for rent. He was too young to live in the government-supported senior district. So there he was, a single man of no benefit to us. A homeless nuisance.

He did it to himself. Why didn't he find another job? How lazy, they taunt and mock and curse. *He can't contribute to the economy. If he's not a consumer, what is he? Worthless.* But, the poor man, he couldn't find a job in time.

When I was little I would ask my mom why the people acted this way.

"Because they're happy it's not happening to them," she would snarl, spit flying from her rounded tongue. Then she would fall to silence, and blink her eyes a lot.

I replied once that I thought ghosts came in from the outside. Mom looked very concerned about this.

"Let's watch them sneak in through the cracks in the door, Mommy."

"Sempra! Where did you hear something like that?" She muttered.

"In a dream." I never mentioned it again.

Sometimes colors grow blurry and slow. That's how I know I've seen it before. In a dream. But Mom says it's just a coincidence. Just a coincidence, of course.

I like to pretend that it's more than that. Then I become unique. Sempra the psychic with prophetic dreams. A mystic in tune with the universe.

Alden says that everyone wants to be recognized in some way, whether consciously or not. That's what drives us to do almost anything. But it's not satisfying unless you deserve it.

That man doesn't deserve to leave. His boss fired him just because he was late.

"Yes, I knew of his condition, " says the mustached employer to a reporter, "but that's no excuse. If he wasn't a good worker, he wasn't a good worker, that's all there is to it. Late every night . . . I'm not going to give him special treatment. He didn't get his act together and he had to pay the consequences. It's not my fault he never found another job."

He has cancer. Soon he'll be dead. I just, I can't help thinking— at least he'll see the outside before he dies. That's bad. I know. It's easy to glorify something you know nothing about. Then you can hold it up above real life. At least, until you find out the truth.

The next night Ms. Morgan lengthens her back in front of the class. Caverns in her withered, fleshy face suck in the lights overhead. Out of them come blunt shadows that float. She cracks her bony neck. It crunches, dead.

"That's why you should stay in school, kids," she tries to laugh but it comes out as a wet cough. "So you can stay in the facility. Need I remind you about the vagrant ways of the outsiders?"

No one answers. I shift around in my metal chair, staring at the barren walls of the minimalist classroom. Anywhere but at my teacher.

"Those barbaric outsiders have lost all sense of morality. They go around strangling each other, and sleep with guns under their pillows. Just to get a hold of the last remnants of civilization. Those people lust after the things we left behind. A bucket. Maybe a can of soup. They're thieves. Filthy, greedy thieves, all of them.

"We are so lucky to have all the things we do. Could you imagine poverty, starvation, war? Without our structured economy you would have no food, no clothes, nowhere to live. Nothing. You don't know how lucky you are."

Alden slams his head down on the table. When Ms. Morgan gets into a rant like this, she doesn't even notice what's happening around her. We call it her trance.

"Those people are slaves to the sun," she goes on. "Here, we are free."

With a heavy pop Alden stands up, knocking back his chair. Our heads turn eagerly towards this disruption. His face remains calm above his tense body, fists clenched. He impatiently nudges away a stray black hair dangling over his low forehead.

"How do you know?" The outline of his jawbone grows more prominent with each word.

"Excuse me?" Ms. Morgan's light brown eyes diminish to slits.

"How does anyone know what's out there?" Alden glances down uneasily at the legs of the fallen chair. "No one sees it. If no one leaves, how do we even know that there are outsiders?"

"It's a matter of science, boy. Something a low-class runt like you will never understand."

We think this is the end of it. It's clear that Ms. Morgan thinks so, too. She clenches her robes to sit down again. The room feels tight. Across the table Greg clears his throat. I consider comforting Alden, but it's impossible to speak. Instead I reach a hand over to lay on his shoulder. But he's still standing. I suddenly notice the long, wiry muscles beneath his bare arms. His chest doesn't move. He's holding his breath.

"Ah, so you don't understand it either."

This doesn't come out as composedly as he intended it. His quiet voice quivers, but it makes an impact. Ms. Morgan's throat and ragged hairline flush to copper. Her gaze slowly scans the table, resting on Timothy, then me. I shrink away, too repulsed for courtesy. A half smile scratches the left side of her cheek.

"We'll see," is all she curtly says.

Alden casually straightens his chair. He sits watching the table. My hand finally finds his shoulder. It's the corner of a dark wall that holds all the knowledge in the world. When the planet tilts some of it is spilled into space. Lost to all. Lost to the future.

We look at each other. I feel as he does, so much at once. Then he shakes his head stiffly and shuts his eyes.

No one talks for the rest of class. Ms. Morgan goes on like nothing has happened. I pretend not to exist.

"Don't worry," I tell Alden on the way to the train, "she just doesn't like being questioned. Of course she's going to react like that. You dared to question her authority, her intelligence. And, by the way, I bet you know way more than her. She doesn't know anything."

He shoves his way ahead of me, arms crossed. I'm about to run to catch up with him when Timothy shows up beside me.

"Is he always like that?" He asks.

"Like what?"

"So passionate? Like back in the classroom?"

"Yeah. I guess he is. He doesn't usually . . . act out, though."

"That's cool," he presses his lips together. "Hey, I've gotta go. Talk to you later."

The back of his head drifts away and I don't care. Right now I need Alden. I jog to my old friend's side.

"Alden," I try to keep up with his swift gait. "Alden, you did the right thing."

His heavy breathing matches each step.

"Alden?"

"Can't you just leave me *alone*? For one second?" He mumbles.

"What. . . ?"

"You have no problem with that the rest of the time, and now when I actually want you to— "

"Are you mad at me?"

We hold up our matching black phones. Train passes flash, blue and gold, on the screen. The man nods and lets us enter the sliding glass train doors.

"Is it because of all the time I've been spending with Timothy?" I ask when the train is moving.

"You're my only friend, Sempra. I hope you know that."

"I'm sorry. I didn't mean to— I wasn't thinking."

What more can be said? I didn't think of my friend's feelings, of how he might feel left out. It's my fault. And what can he do, but ask why he isn't as good as Timothy? Timothy, who is the ceiling when Alden is the ground. I itch my nose with the side of my finger. No one walks with their feet hanging upward.

"Do you want to come over?" I ask him softly. He hasn't come for a long time.

"Sure," he breathes after a long pause. "Why not."

We lay with our backs on the tile floor. Alden's cell phone spurts choppy music between our heads. My own phone dangles above my arms as I search the internet. The living room is warm and comfortable. A fuzzy beige blanket is draped across the couch, a speckled red table lamp shines from the corner. This is nice, I say to myself.

Alden used to come here more often, usually leaving before my mom came home. After awhile we got too used to each other, I guess. We got bored. I've never been to his apartment. He's never invited me. When I asked him why, he scrunched his eyebrows together and said, "You wouldn't like it."

I flip my phone around absently. The governments of all the different facilities run the internet. They make the websites, provide all information. We only see what they want us to. But at least we can reach outside of our own walls to something that, for once, isn't solid.

"Oh, I have one. I wonder why they don't have any windows to the outside," Alden rolls over onto his stomach. "Couldn't they use some sort of sun filtering glass or something? Why is everything all blocked out?"

With quick thumbs I type this into the search engine. The touch-screen buttons rumble as I hit them.

"Nothing. It says, *no results were found.*"

"Hmm, I wonder why," he mutters sarcastically. "You know, I don't think we're going to find anything about *anything*. They want to keep us dumb."

"Yeah, you're right," I sigh. "So what else should we do?"

There's nothing on TV. We've long since beaten all of the free online video games. And we're far too old to play *imaginary* games. The only world we have now is this one. Most of the time I would rather go back to hidden lands buried deep in clouds. That was a better life. Now there's nowhere to go.

"We could go for a walk," I offer.

"Who taught you that? Timothy?" Alden's voice strains.

I sit up and turn off the music. Pocketing my phone, I start toward the door.

"Come on," I turn the dull silver doorknob.

"Come on where? We're not actually going for a walk, are we?"

"Sort of . . . I was thinking we'd go to the perimeter."

"The perimeter? Are you kidding? That's so far, what about your Mom?"

"I need to see it. When are we ever going to see it, Alden? We can take the train to the last stop. It goes pretty close."

He jumps to his feet, rubbing his earlobe.

"Okay, but I'm telling my parents that I'm at your house."

The lights are falling already to their early evening setting. Red is added to pale strings of yellow light. We shuffle nervously beneath them. Our shadows are always the same length, always short and stepped on. I watch the concrete ground. Beige and brown and white shoes drum on its belly. Wandering back from work, everyone holds a blank stare. They don't care about the two of us.

People file off the train, their worn synthetic tunics mottled to ivory. One man's round gut is clothed in bright red. He takes wide steps and bends his elbows as he walks. Next to him is a woman with orange and blue striped hair curled into ringlets. Weaving through the crowd, we finally step up onto the train.

"Sempra!" A familiar voice calls.

My mom is standing behind the half closed doors. I slide behind Alden, trying to hide. She waves her arms, motioning me toward her. Her stern face fades away as the train starts moving. My phone vibrates. Where am I going, she wants to know. I reply that I'm going to Alden's.

Only one other person gets off at the last stop. Squat towers loom over us in the fading light. A distraught food wrapper lies in the road, a mysterious puddle slops outside a door. I don't know where I am. And there's no perimeter in sight.

We ramble in a straight line between buildings, their lofty walls creating a dark tunnel. Windows shine down from well-lit apartments muffled with blinds. Finally a glimmer of curved steel pops out at the end of the alley.

"There it is."

In an energetic trot we run to it. There's no other noise and no other people but us. I place my palms against the wall. It's cold, freezing. Alden looks the silver barrier up and down, mouth straight. We kneel to examine the crack above the ground. Nothing is growing out of it, as we had once hoped.

I press my face to the bolts and screws, trying to smell the outside. All there is is this barricade.

"Well, we're he—"

"It's right there," I interrupt, crossing my arms. "Right outside. Where's that window? The one the old guy covered up? Do you think it's real?"

"It could be anywhere. We'd have to walk around the whole perimeter." He dips his head back to glower at the ceiling.

"Why didn't we come here before? It's so close."

"Yeah, but there's not much to look at."

"It's just the idea of it," I turn away. "That's why we're here."

If only I could see through. Beyond my sight is the answer to every secret. That is the world. And this may be the closest I'll ever get to it. One thick, gray wall away.

How can they tell us that this is it? Don't they think we'll be curious? But I guess everyone starts out wondering. Then they grow up. They move on. Because that's the safe thing to do.

CHAPTER SIX

Timothy layers his hand over mine. Below the black-rimmed balcony, a choir sings. Blazing lights rub crimson color onto the stage, coating its robed inhabitants. Their melancholy voices sift through the theater. Sound lifts up from their boots, writhing and vacant.

The green streaks in Timothy's hair seem to glow in the faint darkness. A lock falls above his narrow cheekbone. Above his lips. I sit up straighter in my pillowed seat, trying to watch the show. Twinkling orbs encircle us and the other balconies. We peer down at striped hair, at brown foreheads. The common people.

I feel him looking at me. He cradles my chin with chapped fingertips. I search for the pupil of his right eye, but it blends in too much. Then Timothy pulls me toward him. Closer and closer, until our lips touch. My face burns, and I'm happy that my olive skin doesn't blush red.

Without thinking, I push off his tight chest, eyes wide. In the back of my mind I smile. Once again he smells of strong, clean mint.

"What's wrong?" Timothy leans forward intently, brow buried in concerned wrinkles.

"What?" I feign deafness.

Now I think. What is wrong? It was my first kiss. Maybe that's it. I'm just in shock. After all, it wasn't entirely unpleasant. Just . . . just different.

"I said, what's wrong?" He raises his voice.

"Oh," I mumble, "I . . . just wasn't expecting that. That's all."

With a deep breath he leans back. I try to hear the music again. But I can't. My eyes involuntarily drift to his direction. Then I lean in, leaving a shy peck on his cheek.

His teeth look whiter than usual when he smiles, when he drops forward to kiss me again. I repeat to myself that I should be enjoying this. And soon I am. With a forced confidence I let my hand drip over the back of his head. A bubble grows between my stomach and my throat.

And then the concert ends. We're the last ones out of the theater. With his arm around my waist we continue down the street, away from the entertainment district. The others shrink into distant specks, and soon it's only our harmonizing footsteps.

"Too bad there isn't a park we could go to," Timothy watches the identical line of buildings stretch on for blocks.

"A . . . park?"

"Yeah," he glances down at me. "You know, an open area with some benches and stuff."

"How do you and Alden know all of this?" I laugh lightly through my nose.

"Alden?" The curved smiling lines around his mouth are especially distinct.

"Oh yeah. He's just full of these random facts. I have no idea where he gets them."

"Hmm? Like what?"

"I don't know . . . I guess you'd have to be there."

Silence comes over us for a moment. I swallow, making a gulping noise. Timothy ignores it. We keep on like this for some time. Walking, just walking. It's not uncomfortable. It just is.

I try to feel pride in the fact that I've finally sat in the balcony. All those years I looked up nervously, wondering who was gazing back down. They might as well have spit on us from up there. They could have.

"It was interesting, Miss Sempra," he smiles. "Always interesting."

We come to my street. I didn't know we could walk so far. Timothy grabs both my hands very tenderly. One more kiss. Then he leaves, just as the lights reach their lowest setting.

I stroll to the elevator as slowly as possible, hands resting in my pockets. A young woman with half her head shaved stands alone. Her oval, orange eyes rest on me then fling back to her phone. There are only two elevators in the stark beige lobby. We wait for the same one.

Smeared fingerprints shine on the silver doors. A stolid ding resounds. The young woman steps on without looking up. I capture the opposite corner of the tiny box. It takes too long to move between floors. I wonder if I should say something, but it's too late for a greeting. Then she brushes back her long, lopsided hair. Something glimmers in her ear. Something round.

"What's that?" I come out with it, staring pointedly at her earlobe.

"Oh," she fondles the golden stub between her thumb and pointer finger, "that's my earring."

"It's so different. Where did you—"

The doors open. It's her floor. She rushes out like something is pushing her, stopping only to absently wave.

"See ya," she says.

I've seen piercings before, in pictures in our history text. But I thought they had died out a long time ago. Where did she get that done, at the hair salon? Are they coming back in style? Or maybe she's not from around here. What if she's from another facility? I can't believe she can have an earring.

Mom's lying on the couch watching TV when I come in.

"So? How was it?" She lifts her head from the pillow.

"Good."

Too much has happened, too much to put into words. It wouldn't feel right. She can't take these textures inside and translate them. So I stumble into my room, close the blinds, and watch the photo screen blink through its slideshow. And instead I tell my father.

After school I ask Alden and Timothy about the earring.

"Where could she have gotten it?"

"The government probably snuck into her apartment and stabbed a hole in her ear while she was sleeping. They've marked her," Alden smugly replies.

"Marked her for what?" Timothy doesn't look into Alden's eyes, only at his nose.

"I don't know. Maybe she's next on their list. Maybe she committed a crime, so she's the next to go."

"But no one ever commits any *crimes*," I shake my head.

"No, they do. They just don't get caught," Timothy raises his eyebrows.

"Well it still doesn't make sense," I bounce my gaze back and forth between my two friends. "Why didn't they just kick her out if she did something wrong? That can't be it."

"Wait, what do you mean 'they just don't get caught'?" Alden turns to Timothy and crosses his arms.

"There are people out there who don't follow the rules. And I'm not talking about just ignoring the government's suggestions. I'm talking about trespassing, fraud, stealing. Big stuff."

"And how do you know?"

"All it takes is some simple observation."

Alden glares at Timothy but keeps his mouth closed. We discuss more earring theories, secret societies versus runaway convicts from alien facilities, until we come to the train. Timothy never rides with us. He kisses me goodbye, quickly and dryly, his hand warming my lower back. This is completely normal until I catch Alden's empty eyes staring at us.

By the time I get home there is a hole in my stomach. I just want to sit down, to stop thinking. So I turn on the TV wall and lean against the couch's soft cushions. Mom comes in from work, she asks what's wrong. With a muffled voice I tell her that I don't know.

We watch the wall together. The resolution on the TV is so fine it looks real. It stretches over the square plane of the wall; it *is* the wall. Colors from the screen flicker and dance off of our faces.

"Cheer up," she says lightly during a commercial. "You're not still in a mood about the sun, are you?"

"I'm not in a moo—"

"Oh wait, *shhh,* it's back on."

Sighing heavily, I push myself up from the couch and reach my arms in front of me. Mom doesn't even turn her head from the TV. I shuffle into the hallway, away from our apartment, down the elevator. In an empty corner of the lobby I stand and wait. I wait for the lady with the earring.

A young man bounds in, blonde hair flailing. Then comes a weathered woman with square glasses, a handsome couple with matching purple pants, a man with yellowed teeth. All have vacant earlobes.

With my eyes on the floor I walk to the elevator, ready to give up. Footsteps click from behind me. White shoes pause to my left. Above them stands a cylinder of white topped by a shiny stub.

"Hey," I excitedly disrupt the silence. "Hey, it's you! I— I'm sorry, but I have to ask you. Where did you get your earring?"

"Look, kid, I don't quite know what the government thinks of piercings, so you'll have to keep quiet about it. Got it?" She runs her fingers through the long side of her hair.

"Of course. I won't say a word, I promise."

The elevator opens, throwing out a chattering pair of women. We board the swollen metal room, waiting until the doors close before we continue.

"Really, I won't tell anyone. I know what it's like to hide something from the government," I plead. "Please, I have to know. It's been killing me—"

"Okay, okay. I know I'm asking for it by *wearing* this damn thing. You seem trustworthy. Not like I'm a great judge of character, though, after what happened with Marty. Ugh. Okay, just . . . just whatever. If you *must* know, if you're gonna *die* if you don't find out, I'll just tell you. This earring was passed down through my family. It's *pret-ty* damn old," her high cheekbones rise as she laughs.

"But where did you have—"

"The piercing done? Come on, you think I could get this *done* somewhere? I did it myself. It's called ingenuity, kid. Ingenuity. Try it sometime. It'll get you somewhere."

CHAPTER SEVEN

I sift through the kitchen's stainless steel drawers. They rattle with silverware, bowls, some old scissors. But no needles. Frantically, I search the dusty cabinet in the bathroom, the sparse cupboard above the washing machine.

"What are you looking for, sweetie?"

"Nothing, Mom. Um. We don't have any sewing needles, do we?"

"No. Sempra, what's this about?" She leans against the doorway to the laundry room.

"Nothing. Just a school project about . . . about ancient tools," I slide past her.

"Oh," Mom frowns.

In my bedroom I stroke my soft earlobes, wondering what they would feel like with tiny circles in them. It's not like I have an earring to put in, anyway. Unless I left in the needle as the earring . . .

Maybe there are other ways to be unique. Ways that don't involve bright specks of blood. A new hair color? A fake tattoo drawn on with blue marker? I need something that will assert my independence. Something that says . . . I am *me*.

As I sleep I dream without color. Dark eyelids blink all around me. They wobble on their legs and mumble in deep tones of anguish. I know they'll fall over if I yell, but I can't speak, because the universe hasn't been born yet. Instead I look down and notice that

I'm falling. Guttural yelps brush past me on either side, coming from beyond what I can see.

Then I'm holding a splintering wooden spear, and feel a rush of desire to hurl the crude weapon into a waving ball of light. I know instinctively that this should be the sun, but it's not. It blisters and festers, a thing of hatred that needs to be destroyed. So, with a sense of dread, I throw the spear.

What have you done, my mom gasps. *You killed the womb. You killed the womb. How will the Earth grow now*? She steps in front of me and shakes me by the shoulders. But it's not my mom anymore. It's the man with the gray slanted eyes.

We float behind a lady with long hair, so long that it encircles us. Reaching out, I pet the strand nearest me, its soft, fine waves. They move like water. She glimpses back at us and I panic. Her face is terrifying, though I can't see it. I don't want to go with her anymore; wherever we're going, we won't come back.

Nothing more exists, the lady grimaces. Her voice is a painful crash after years of silence. *This is the edge of the universe.* The man holds my head from behind my ears, forcing me to look. But I can't look over the edge. It hurts, it burns, it would be death. Instead, I wake up.

After this dream I don't want to go back to sleep. Then I might dream again. Do you dream when you're dead? If there's an afterlife, is it just like this one, with sleeping and dreams? That would be pointless. Why would a god, a creator, bother making death if it is just a reflection?

Sometimes I wonder what life is for. Is it just scientific chance? Or is there some purpose that we have as conscious beings? Does there need to be?

I wish I had the book. It would be nice to be away right now, to drift away from the masked window and the corners ripe with wooly shadows. Everything ticks in the daytime. Staccato notes weave through the air, restless.

When I was little I would watch TV when I couldn't sleep. I'd sneak out to the living room and put it on mute. It was the light that I liked. And, to see other people, it felt like someone was there. When everyone else is asleep it's hard not to feel all alone.

Placing each foot softly on the cold floor, I crack my door open and creep out to the couch. There's a rerun of an old series on, a historical drama about the first generation of the facility. The founders sit on thrones in the newly finished governmental district. Handsome with stubble on their chins, they guide the people justly but sternly from their concrete terrace.

Their mouths shift as they shout commands to their workers. A woman, painted blonde, lays a gentle hand on the shoulder of one of the founders. I shut my eyes to let the light leak through.

"Sempra, what did I tell you about falling asleep with the TV on?" Is how my mom wakes me up that night.

I sit up slowly. With a tired grunt I adjust the wrinkled legs of my pajama pants, I scoop a hair away from my face. Then there is toast flavored mush, there is tying my hair into a high ponytail. And we leave to complete our societal duties.

During class I try to imagine other worlds. Alden stares at his bony hands. Timothy's gaze keeps flipping from Ms. Morgan to me.

"Want to come over?" He whispers just as everyone stands up at the bell.

"Sure."

We rush out before Alden can ask us where we're going. Holding hands, we walk parallel to the train towards a living district. I've never been to Timothy's apartment. The building looks just like mine, just like all the others. Square, gray, laced with small windows. Even the lobby is identical.

"Well, this is it," he holds the door for me when we get to the top floor.

It's spacious, far bigger than mine. There's a gold, velvet couch in the sitting room. A polished glass table sits in the adjoining dining room with matching chairs for six. Above them dangles a chandelier that glimmers against red walls. The floors are clothed in mauve, tasseled rugs. On everything clings the scent of cinnamon.

"Wow."

Usually I try to forget that he's rich. It makes me feel inadequate, or something, like he shouldn't have chosen me because I'm not in his class. But he doesn't care about things like that. So I guess I shouldn't either.

A frail woman crowned by red hair mixed with spits of white walks in from the kitchen. She folds her hands in front of her beige blouse.

"Oh, Sempra, this is our housekeeper, Macy," Timothy motions to each of us in turn.

"Nice to meet you, Sempra," Macy shakes my hand warmly. "Would either of you like anything to eat or drink?"

Timothy looks at me expectedly.

"Um, no thanks, I'm fine."

Macy smiles complacently with her neck extended gracefully. I realize that, though she's older, her face is still very pretty.

"Alright, let me know if you need anything." Still smiling, she shuffles back into the kitchen.

A housekeeper. A housekeeper, for an apartment? No one lives in mansions anymore. I didn't think anyone would need someone to clean or cook for them in such a small space. But if you're rich, why waste any of your time with housework when you don't have to?

We sit on the couch watching the TV wall. They're showing one of the final presidential debates between Kern Bradley and Harmond Nielson. The candidates discuss taxes, the government's control, the educational system. A man in the audience holds up the back of an old shirt on which he's scrawled, *a vote for Bradley is a vote for freedom*, in red marker.

"Who do you think's gonna win?" Timothy asks with his arm slung around me.

"Mmm. I don't know. Probably Natalia's dad."

"But who do you want to win?"

"I . . . haven't even thought about it, really. Does it matter?" I laugh dryly. "We can't even vote yet, anyway."

With his mouth barely cracked open he squints at me.

"Yeah, we're all just a bunch of powerless *children*, right?" He snorts. "So, you wanna watch something else?"

"Alden says that TV is an excuse not to think. It sucks you in and you just absorb it for hours. And no one even questions it. They just go along with it and rush to the screen as soon as they get home."

"It's funny, Sempra," Timothy leans forward, pulling his arm from my back. "You could probably be considered one of those people."

His face is passive in the eyes, but full in the mouth. Thin lips curl and long nostrils flare. He looks like he's trying not to smile. I give him a confused shake of the head but say nothing. My eyes find the floor, tracing swirled lines in the carpet.

"I mean," he goes on, "you kind of just go along with what Alden tells you. How much thinking have you actually done?"

The way he says it, like he's trying to be gentle. God. It makes me want to punch something. To run. To scream. To scrape the world apart with my fingernails. Standing up I knock my shin on the glass coffee table. I keep my features flat and pretend it doesn't throb. I pretend that I don't want to pick up that table and throw it out the window.

"I have to go." He doesn't deserve composure. Why should I pretend that I'm not mad when I am? I want him to deal with what he's done.

"I— I didn't mean it that way, I just—"

"See you tomorrow," I shut the door heavily and storm out to the hallway.

Who is he to say that? Who is he?

I board the train while pushing tears away. There are three unread texts on my phone. *Where are you*, reads the first. *Are you riding the train?* And, finally, *Ok. I'm leaving without you.* Oh, Alden.

Half of me hates Alden because Timothy is right. Alden is the one who does all the thinking. But the other half of me wants to cling to the friend who I grew alongside from childhood. Alden would never insult me. He's too kind, too soft. It's Timothy who's the problem.

The apartment is empty and I'm glad. Finally, I let the tears escape. They rest on the bridge of my nose. Bitterly, I wipe them on my bedspread. I feel dumb. Dumb, insulted, betrayed. And, most of all, alone.

Am I overreacting? I *do* think. Just because I don't spout off my thoughts every few seconds like Alden does . . .

It's true. It's true. He's right. I take what Alden says because it's different, it's clever. And by repeating it I try to steal those qualities for myself. Really, I'm nothing but a follower.

Now I feel like I've lost something.

The lights still eagerly beam through the window, but it feels like day. It's hollow, made from foam that's been burnt black. Briefly, I wonder what the facility would look like if the electricity failed. Dark, I'd suppose. Like crisp nothing. What chaos would ensue, everyone bumping into everything. We would be helpless. Blind and helpless. Seems to me we should worship the electricians.

A gravelly voice pushes through the closed walls of my room. The front door claps shut. Another voice enters.

"Sempra! Sempra!"

Oh great.

"Now, where is that little granddaughter of mine," the voice huffs absently to my mom.

"Sempra, come out here and say hello to your grandmother," Mom commands.

Grandma hasn't come to visit for a few months. She's usually too busy dying her friends' hair over in the senior district. That's where we all go when we become old. Alden says that's when . . . never mind.

Sometimes my grandma comes and stays a few nights with us. Mom usually invites her when she starts to feel lonely. Grandma is the cure for Mom's aversion to solitude.

Silently, sullenly, I leave my bedroom.

"Oh *there* you are. Goodness, all the time these kids spend in their rooms these days. Come, give Grandma a hug," she holds out arms wrapped in light, eggshell fabric. Every color imaginable streaks her bobbed hair.

"Hi Grandma."

We all shift into the kitchen. For once the third chair is occupied. It's usually nice to have another person around, at least for the first few hours. But today I just want to hide.

My mom and grandma talk, but I don't listen. I can't think of anything except what Timothy said to me earlier. The incident, I call it.

Grandma's mouth is too wet. It makes a slopping noise when she opens it. I can't help but stare at her polished, crooked, teeth.

"So, Sempra, dear," Grandma taps on the table with her index finger, "what have you been up to lately?"

She waits kindly for an answer. Her eyes are stretched too wide beneath her round glasses. After a second of buzzing silence, I answer.

"School, homework . . . reading."

"What about that boy you've been seeing? What's his name?" Grandma smiles slyly.

"How did you know about that?" I throw my mom a look of savage distaste.

"He's a rich one, isn't he? Is he handsome?"

"I don't know about him anymore," my words are heavy with melancholy.

"Ah, well. There'll be a whole line of 'em waiting out the door for you in a few years, you wait and see," she steadily watches my face, sparse eyebrows curled inward. "Now, what happened to you hair?"

"What do you mean?" I grab a fist of my thick, dark tresses.

"It's gotten so long," she rubs a strand between her fingers, "and when was the last time you colored it?"

"It looks...*natural*," my mom leans into the table, her chin in her hands.

I don't know how she means this, whether it's good or bad. But I smile, and I nod, because it's perfect. In each blink I see the woman in my dream. Beneath her clouded visage, I begin to recognize my own reflection.

CHAPTER EIGHT

"Can you believe it?" Alden peers up at me when I walk into the classroom.

"What?"

"Didn't you see the news? Kern Bradley is gone. They got rid of him," his voice is forcibly stale.

I collapse to my seat. Our apprehensive classmates inaudibly mumble, they huddle together, biting their lips. Natalia is missing. So is Timothy. Almost shaking, I wrap my hands over my mouth. Slowly, I count my warm breaths. Alden looks even thinner than usual.

"You mean . . . they kicked him out? To the outside?" I finally manage. "How can they do that?"

"They're the government. They control everything," he shakes his head. "So why would they let a radical win the election if they don't have to?"

As Ms. Morgan grimly lectures us, I turn over in my mind what this really means. Everything has changed. Here we are, true slaves to a dictatorship. The only other option is near death.

Why did they ever let us vote in the first place? It's always been them, the same group, the descendants of our wealth-laden founders. They hold all the power. Now fear is starting to slice each of us into half-people. We are nothing but guests in their kingdom.

Timothy bursts in, panting and late. His brown eyes go right to me, smiling. It takes me a moment to remember that I'm mad at him. Ms. Morgan says nothing. She marches him out to the hall-way, shutting the door briskly behind them. The rest of us return to our thoughts.

The class jumps when they suddenly come back in. Timothy finds his place beside me, slouching in the shoulders. He grabs my hand, and I want to forgive him. What's happened is so much worse than what he said to me.

"Sempra," he whispers, "I'm sorry. About what I said. I just wanted to push you to go beyond just being smart, because I know you can."

Ms. Morgan glares pointedly at me, ignoring the fact that Timo-thy is the one making noise. We feign decorum until she turns to her phone.

"It's okay," I barely utter sound.

Class goes by with pronounced frowns on most of our faces. I feel as though a darkness is starting to enshroud me like a satin hood. The square window on the edge of the room shows another empty room beyond it. And another. And another. It's a ghost that slides under us so we don't have to feel each step as we walk.

We are forced to hear again of the flaws of our predecessors' materialism, of the brilliance of our sustainable lifestyle, of the im-portance of stimulating the economy. Ms. Morgan only makes one comment concerning the greatest upset in our recent history.

"I do hope you're keeping up with your current events," she raises her leaded eyebrow wisps.

I'm sure she's secretly pleased that one less person will live the dream she never could. If she had become president, she would never have given back that power, either. President Morgan, the im-mortal, vicious tyrant.

Alden and I and Timothy journey away from the school. My eyes seem to have been sucked waterless. They burn and itch, mak-ing me tired. All of me is tired.

"So what did Ms. Morgan say to you outside the classroom?" Alden asks Timothy.

"Oh, uh, nothing, really," Timothy shrugs, watching the buildings we've spent our lives passing by.

"Tardiness will not be accepted, young man," I mimic Ms. Morgan's high tone. "Don't let this happen again, or you'll be expelled."

"Exactly. Like I said, *nothing*," Timothy laughs with a seriousness in his eyes.

We part ways. Soon I drift silently into my apartment, wary of facing my grandmother. I have one foot safely in my bedroom when she bounces out of the kitchen.

"There's my little Sempra! How was school today?"

I give her a genuine but swift hug, stretching my arms around her plump belly.

"It was good," I lie.

With a fake smile draped over my mouth, I force myself to spend ten long minutes chatting with her. Then, with the excuse of homework, I hide in my room. I need to think. To sort things out.

The front door taps shut, bringing forth my mom. Mom and Grandma greet each other with boisterous ferocity. They murmur contentedly for awhile. The bright clang of dishes mingles with their voices.

"Oh, this whole thing. It just reminds me so much of what happened to that poor husband of yours," my grandmother pronounces loud enough to be heard through my door.

"*Shhh,*" Mom quiets her wildly. I prop my ear against the door. "She doesn't know."

"Wha— I thought you were going to tell her when she turned sixteen. Her birthday was months ago!"

My lips part open as I watch the white door with sweaty hands.

"I . . . I just couldn't, Mom. The way she talks about the outside . . . If she really knew what happened to her father, if she really knew what he did . . . I'm just worried she would go too far."

"Mom, what are you talking about?" I yell helplessly from my open doorframe.

"Come here," Grandma places a hand over my mom's closed fist, unraveling her soft fingers. "Your mother will tell you."

Suddenly I feel like a little kid. I sit down in my usual chair and cross my legs. The metal table needs cleaned. It has smudges around its corners.

"Sempra. The year you were born," my mother sighs, closing her eyes. "The year you were born, your father was exiled from the facility."

That can't be right. He's dead, he's been dead for so long…

"He was an activist," she continues, "trying to give the people more freedoms while diminishing the power of the government. But it didn't work. They didn't like all his protesting, and…"

She pauses, tears clouding her honey tinted eyes. Grandma grabs her hand tighter.

"They told him that if he left without making trouble, you and I would be allowed to stay. So he did. He left."

It's quiet. The appliances hum. The three of us breathe.

"Don't you think I would've liked to know?" I stand up, growing restless, angry. "Don't you think I would've wanted to know that my father is *still alive*?"

"Sempra, honey, we don't know if he's alive or not," Grandma stammers patiently.

"So you assume he's dead? How could you not tell me, Mom?" My words are carved of broken stones. Everything is hot and whirling. I clap my hands against my skull.

"What did it hurt, not knowing? I mean, really, Sempra. Wouldn't you have looked down on your father for it?" Her words sound rehearsed.

"Looked down on him? How could you think that? I respect him a thousand times more than I have ever respected you!" I stumble into my room and slam the door.

Flopping on my bed, I weep as though my father is newly dead. What deception. My own mother has lied to me for my entire life.

I will choose not to kill him. He could still be out there. Breathing, living, running.

My world is empty with change. Comfort has left all things. I consider running to the perimeter, halfway hoping that Alden might be there. Sensing my distress, he would be waiting with his back to the wall. But that would only bring trouble, at this time of day. Alden is probably asleep, by now, anyway.

What I really want to do is find the window to the outside. It's more than just rotting logs and abandoned shacks out there. It's my father, face to the sky. One way or another.

CHAPTER NINE

Hunger overcomes me, so I finally leave my room. No light pushes under my door. They must be asleep. I glide into the living room, both weightless and heavy, my throat swollen from crying.

The light is still on in the kitchen. My mom sits with her head in her hands at the kitchen table. But when did she grow so old? When did her brown skin pall to gray? I hesitate. My stomach rumbles.

Feeble hands unfold from her eyes.

"Sempra?" She mumbles, her mouth sagging lopsidedly. "Come here, sit down. I need to talk to you."

I reach the table and haul my knees to my chest. Mom's breath has grown stale. Her lips are chapped.

"I should've told you. I'm sorry," she finds my eyes, shaking her head with a slow sadness. "I'm so sorry. It's all I can say. And no matter how many times I say it, it will never be enough."

"Why didn't you go with him? How could you let him disappear?" My voice is rough after hours of hibernation.

"When he left, he took my heart with him. I held on to his arm for days, begging to go with him, trying desperately to convince him that we would have a better chance of surviving the unknown if we were together. All of that.

"But then he made me promise not to follow him. For you, Sempra. So you would have a better life. If I didn't have you to live for, I would've left a long time ago."

Something in me begins to understand. My mom's feelings are suddenly a tangible thing. I release my knees and cross my ankles.

"I'm old enough now. We should go, go after him. He could still be out there, Mom."

"Oh, Sempra," she lets out a long, sighing, wind. "We can't. You know we can't."

"Why? Why not? What's so impossible about it?"

"It's too dangerous. And there's no guarantee . . . He could be anywhere in the world, if he's even alive at all."

Now they're unraveling, the thoughts that were just beginning to make sense. Who is this woman, this humble coward? Her eye sockets are purple, the capillaries on her nose twitch blindly. She looks like she has lived without any life. Her own personal sun beneath her chest is dimmed, dormant.

"You would do anything for him if you really loved him."

"Everything sounds easier when you're young," her tone is still soft, even as I'm screaming at her.

"I'll go. I'll do it," I stand up.

"There's no coming home once you've left."

"So you think I'd miss being a slave imprisoned in a box? What should I do, then? Just go along with whatever those idiots say?"

"Yes. Move on, block out what bothers you. Concentrate on yourself, on your own life. Not on them. There's nothing we can do. Okay? Things aren't so bad, here. We have everything we need."

I stare at her as a novel being. My mouth is tired of words. My mind is out of breath.

"I made a promise, Sempra, and I intend to keep it. This was the life he wanted for us," she hugs me across the shoulders. "Take it or leave it."

We go to bed. My hunger has disappeared. I want to fall asleep so that everything will stop. Finally, it does.

When I arrive at school I tell Alden and Timothy of my plan to leave the facility.

"But you can't go," Alden ejects without even a pause. "I don't think I could handle any of this without you."

Timothy blinks solidly at the ground. He rotates his chair so it's parallel to the table. His face is stiff, unmoving. It almost reminds me of my mother's.

Class goes on as usual in our small, gray world. My father saw it that way too, if he was trying to change things. He's become a puzzle. I wonder what he would really want me to do. There's a difference, I suppose, between changing our world and leaving it.

"So you really want to leave us?" Alden asks with his hands in his pockets.

"No. Not you. I want to leave all of *this*," I motion to the narrow street we follow to the train.

"Sempra," Timothy, who's been silent all night, grabs my hand. "I still feel bad about what I said. It's been killing me. Will you come with me, so I can make it up to you?"

"Can Alden come?" I glance uneasily at my friend. He grimaces and inches backward.

"No, it's okay. I have to go. Have fun," Alden walks away with his head hanging.

Timothy makes everything seem in place. Like all is all, and not nothing, anymore. Part of me might be falling in love with him. Part of me just *wants* to.

Through bare shadows we swim. The tallest building in the facility stretches high above the business district. It's a copy of all the others, only closer to the ceiling. This was the first building in the facility. It exhausted too many resources, so they decided to make the other ones smaller.

I've been to the top of it. I thought everyone had. But this is where Timothy leads me for his great surprise. So I smile. And I pretend I'm excited to touch the artificial sky. We climb six stories of metal stairs leading up its side. They seem never to end.

Finally, our thighs burning, we reach the top.

"Here we are," Timothy's fingers dust the bolted ceiling. "On top of the world."

Standing against the fenceless edge, I look down on the city. The lights sparkle like I imagine stars would.

"It's nice."

But not enough. It's never enough when I know there's more.

Timothy kisses me on the cheek, his arm warming my shoulders.

"I've always loved it up here. It's beautiful . . . *You're* beautiful. Everyone says that rich girls are the prettiest, but one look at you would prove them wrong, Miss Sempra."

"Why..." I giggle. "Why is it that you always call me Miss Sempra?"

"I don't know. I just like the way it sounds." He pulls me into his chest.

"Well, I agree. It really is quite *dapper*, Mr. Timothy."

Then his lips bond to mine, gently and passionately. I wonder if I have known him in another life. It seems impossible that death has or will ever come. The air systems whisper. The lights hum. But, for all I know, eternity could be above me, anyway.

His nails scratch against the back of my neck as he pulls away from me. We let the view distract us for a moment.

"Something's been bothering you. Something more than what President Nielson did, or what I said," he pauses. "You can tell me anything, you know."

But I know that I can't. I can't tell anyone about my father. Not even Alden. It would then be spoken into unbreakable existence.

"I'm okay, everything's fine."

Time passes with nothing said. My face is shocked into a smile built of stone. What are we doing here, pondering below a ceiling, amidst an artificial view? How easy it would be to open the door and just go. It would only be difficult to let your dependence fade.

What is out there, really? Is there air to breathe? Water to sip? Or are there miles of ancient streambeds cracked dry in the aching heat? Are the stories true, of savage outsiders and a merciless sun?

And freedom? What of that?

"Do you think I should do it?" I break the silence.

"What?"

"Leave the facility. Go to the outside."

"That's suicide!" He contemplates me with narrowing concern, his brow furrowed. "Why do you think people came here in the first place? The sun is too strong, it would kill you eventually. Why would you want to do something that could kill you?"

"I don't know . . . I mean, isn't everyone nocturnal anyways? If the outsiders live out there, I could too, there must be a way," I slip two fingers through my thick hair. "Haven't you ever wondered what's really out there?"

"Of course. And, you know, I'm curious about what it's like after you die, too, but that doesn't mean I'm gonna try it. It's just —if you don't like it, there's no coming back," Timothy tilts his sullen face down.

"That's why I'm still here," I mumble, grasping his thumb playfully.

We sway down the staircase, parting ways at the bottom. The lights are dimming already, and the work rush is over. Washed bare are the streets. Emptier still is the glistening, seat-less train. It occurs to me that, really, this is how things usually are.

There is no one waiting for me in the apartment. Mom must be accompanying my grandmother home. I forgot she was leaving so soon. All of this must have been too much for her. Now she'll sit in a plush chair by the window, chatting with the other old people about television stars, about the best hair brushing methods.

Never once will they mention their age, or that they're going to die soon. Their foreheads, stroked by wrinkled flaps, alert everyone of this. So why would they talk about it? We all die. It's nothing new. The only thing that matters is *when*.

CHAPTER TEN

Natalia is back at school. If anyone else had missed a week, they would be unhesitatingly expelled. Being the dictator's daughter certainly has it's upsides.

She's draped in pale gray; a humble, silken blouse with matching slacks. The top of her scalp is sliced with long rows where the teeth of a comb have spent hours.

Here she is, with anything she could ever want. With unequivocal wealth and power. Her life will be royal blue tunics. Jeweled, golden phone covers. Why is she here, glancing uneasily up and down the table, wearing only a shade darker than the impoverished?

If she could be something else, she would be dead grass, I think. Not green grass like in old photos. No, something more like the faded pages of *The Call of the Wild*. Dry, crumbling away at the slightest touch. Blades of it cover her face in a mask. They're meant to make us forget, to filter away undeclared blame.

The rest of us sink away from her. It's like we've already abandoned her. We've grown years since she's been hiding from us.

Ms. Morgan only nods to Natalia, exuding cold courtesy. You can't tell what's inside either of them. Maybe Natalia will become a teacher someday. I could see her floating in front of the room in a purple gown, herding us lower-class kids beneath the table with a glossy, braided whip.

Then she looks at me, without scowling, without even seeing. Ropes of arid tears dangle below the black circles in her eyes.

As I cross through the doorway to leave, she pushes me down the hall. Now she sees me.

"You know, Sempra, I don't always approve of what my dad is doing," she barks defensively, tearing her hand away from my shoulder.

I maintain a shocked silence. A few of our classmates saunter backwards, both staring and making their escape. Alden and Timothy hover next to the door. In the flat hallway light, Natalia's face contorts with dull insanity.

"Look," she crosses her arms, "I know what everyone thinks. But I'm not him. I didn't want this any more than you did."

Before I can respond, Natalia leans forward, newly calm. She smells like heavy wax. Within her grave expression there is no room for scorn.

"I know you don't like me very much, but I have to warn you, Sempra. You're on my dad's list. I don't know what for, but...you'd better be careful."

It must be because of my father. They're keeping an eye on the rebel's daughter.

"Thanks . . . thanks for telling me," is all I can think to say.

She lunges away as quickly as she came, her back stiffening as she walks. I join my friends with my hands shoved in my pockets. Timothy's mouth creeps into a half smile.

"What was that all about?" Pity soaks his voice. As though I can't handle Natalia. As though she's too much for me.

"I have no idea. She wasn't making any sense." How can I tell them when they don't know about my father? Better to just brush it off, move on.

Halfway to the train Alden stops suddenly. He's been quiet lately. His eyes are red where they should be white.

"Sempra," he lets his arms droop at his sides, lifting his chin up proudly. "If you leave, I mean, if you go to the outside . . . I'll go with you."

Oh, Alden. He's really been worried about this, hasn't he. We stand there in the middle of the street, a hushed triangle.

"Do you really mean that?" I laugh breathily.

"Just tell me when we're leaving."

"Same with me. I'd go too," Timothy hastily adds, growing quieter with each word.

"You know what? I think that, for now at least, I'm staying."

As soon as I say it I feel like I'm abandoning my father. To my friends, I've simply decided to postpone a daring adventure. Maybe it's partially that. But, really, I've succumbed to the cowardice of my mother.

How easy it is to say things. Action is what solidifies you as a person. Here are two choices, stay or go. Easy or hard. Perhaps even life or death. It's not that simple, I know. Nothing is. Still, I've made the choice that others want.

"What made you change your mind?" Alden runs to my side.

Shrugging, I peer up at Timothy through a wall of sprawling hair. His light brown neck pops against the white collar of his tunic. Small, round eyes hold my gaze, and I want to sigh— with longing, with contentment, with a peculiar nostalgia. But I don't.

"Oh, I don't know. Maybe things aren't as bad as I thought they were."

I don't really expect them to come with me. And I don't want them to. If we really did it, if we really left and were ambushed with disaster . . . it would be my fault. All my fault. Death by sun. Thirsting to death in the dark, freezing night. Quiet starvation. Being pierced through the heart with an outsider's rusted bullet. All of it.

So this is what I choose for myself. Until it's the right time. Until the forgiving presence of someday.

CHAPTER ELEVEN

Meet me at the top of the tallest building after school, says the text message. *I have something to show you.*

Timothy isn't in class. He's probably not sick if he wants to meet up with me later. Alden scans the text over my shoulder. I pretend not to notice.

Facing me from across the table is Natalia. Every few minutes she lets one eye peek up at me, before returning to the art of avoidance. Her attempt at kindness has caused her to hate me even more. It embarrassed her, I think. She holds her phone gingerly, like she's afraid of bending her wrists.

Ms. Morgan is gone today, too. A young substitute lounges in her high-backed chair at the front of the room. Her name is Mrs. George. The first thing she does is laugh through her nose about how she has a man's first name as a last name.

"No wonder it's called a sir-name," she bites her petite bottom lip, slapping her palms against broad thighs.

After calling us kiddos she orders us to read the next two chapters of *A Confluence of Steel.* Then she winks.

She's a remarkably pale beige, next to someone as dark brown as Alden. Pale and chubby. Beneath her flat, gaping nostrils is a chin that crumbles into her wide neck. Down the table, Greg hasn't even blinked, he's so mesmerized with her.

The classroom loses its studious tone within seconds. Wisps of murmured conversation agitate the once static air.

As I'm replying to Timothy's text, Mrs. George strolls to my seat with plump hands clasped behind her back.

"That doesn't look half as interesting as what you're *supposed* to be reading," she grunts.

I flip back to the e-book, but don't offer her any vocal reply. Why me, when no one else is reading either? The other kids heed my warning. Silence pulls over us.

From her throne at the head of the table, the substitute frowns at me. Soon I don't feel her eyes touching me anymore. Her pallid eyelids are stretched down. She's asleep.

Bret, the second wealthiest in the class, jumps up. His yellow and red spiked hair sparkles with an oily sheen.

"Finally!" He yells too loudly, standing on his chair.

With arms flailing to the ceiling, all the rich kids follow his lead. They giggle like they've shrunken to half their age. Alden doesn't even smile. Greg pokes Natalia in the stomach, and she shrieks. Mrs. George's eyes fly open.

She only stares, seemingly unable to comprehend the scene in front of her. Then her full cheeks squint into a grin. And she laughs.

"Oh, you kiddos. Come on, come on, sit down, everyone," she sputters. "Sit down, now. Boy, do you all remind me of me when I was a kid."

Her back faces our side of the table for the rest of class.

Alden rushes out ahead of me. He turns his head quickly around, waving goodbye. Only his mouth wears the distress he's trying to conceal.

Something feels different outside of the school. I can't place it. Above are the golden lights. Around are the angular buildings. Below is the aged, trampled pavement. But where is that sound? That distant ticking? When did the stillness spread?

Quickly, I make my way to the tallest building. How odd it feels to be walking alone. Maybe I should've asked Alden to come. But Timothy didn't invite him . . . he never does.

Soon I arrive at the endless staircase. Its metallic limbs embrace the side of the building with a stolid certainty. I jog upon their small, fat universes. My arms sweep against my waist. By the time I get to the top, all breath has been crushed out of me.

There is Timothy, standing with a folded pillowcase crossed between his forearms. He shifts the white package to one hand.

"There you are," he pulls me towards him. Now, more than ever, he smells of mint.

"Here I am," I pant.

We kiss, brushing fingertips against smooth, russet features. He holds me so gently. Like I'm only air. It's not being up above that swells my chest. It's not even being away. Timothy's the only one who could make me forget that there's an Earth beneath us.

"What's that?" I nod to the rectangle wrapped in cloth.

"Oh, this," he reaches into the pillowcase. "This is what I wanted to show you."

Out of white creases comes a rectangle. On its blue cover the words *Brave New World* are strewn. Time seems to freeze. After a moment I realize this is paper. Pages.

"Another one," I stroke the thick, white letters spelling *Aldous Huxley* .

Timothy's gaze jumps from the book to me.

"What do you mean, another one?" He waits, but I don't reply. I draw back my arms, as though the book has burnt me. "You mean you've seen one of these before?"

Oh no, oh no. My first thought is to run away. Take it back. Throw the book over the edge. Something. How could I be so stupid, to speak my thoughts aloud?

"Never mind," I mumble without looking up. But I hesitated for too long. He saw my regretful grimace. Even I can hear the fear in my voice.

"Sempra, it's okay. You can tell me. You can tell me anything, remember?"

In his eyes I find nothing but sincerity. Is that enough? Can I trust him with the secret that entangles Alden and me? But what is more is, do I love him now? If I love him, I have to tell him. And if he loves me, it will be his secret, too. Maybe it already is.

So I whisper of the time when Alden first showed me our treasure. How I read it all in one dawn. Timothy gasps when I say Alden found it abandoned on the street. That's where he got his, too.

"*The Call of the Wild*," I sing, "is the best book in the world."

"Just wait until you read *Brave New World*," Timothy grins. "I'll let you borrow it when I'm finished."

CHAPTER TWELVE

"Sempra..." cuts a heavy voice through vanishing dreams. "Sempra, wake up."

Angrily, I respond without opening my eyes. It's our monthly night off from school. The *one time* I get to sleep in. "What? What is it?" I scowl, pulling up my blanket.

She exhales, shifting her weight creakily. Then nothing. Did she leave? I peek over the hem of my beige sheets. My mom stands contemplating the window with one thumb pressed to her bottom lip.

"It's your friend, Alden," her eyebrows curve into jagged lines. "He's . . . he's . . . I just saw them dragging him down the street . . . they —"

Run, run, run. I have to run. Have to catch up to him. Holding my breath, I thrust on shoes. Then I'm leaping down the hall, into the infuriating elevator. In my delicate, white pajamas I sprint through the streets. Sweat bathes my underarms, my forehead. But I can't stop. Can't think.

There's no cheering. They're still waking up. It's just me, chasing sulking shadows to the door.

A small crowd protrudes from a block away. I shove elbows and shoulders and unknown body parts with unfeeling vigor. Get out of my way, I want to yell. All of you! You ignorant, sadistic bastards. These are not people. Just bodies. They are mirrors to dusty bricks.

But I can't speak. With hope and grief mingling in each pace, I run.

Then I see him. Thin wrists rimmed with bulky metal. Burly guards gripping his weak, brown arms. Like they want to crack them between their bleached, bulbous teeth. What ease caresses their shallow jaws, these who have given what they think and know to be death.

Trembling, I trail them all the way to the door. Always they are just ahead of me. Alden's floppy black hair is all I can focus on. He's not scared, I know he's not.

This is the longest path they could take. They like to parade those who are exiled through the facility, as though they're proving a point.

I've never seen the door to the outside. When I do, I'm wet and shaking, spitting a lock of hair from my mouth.

"Alden!" I hoarsely, desperately scream.

When his head turns I start to cry. Oh, Alden, *Alden*. None of this is real. It can't be. Frozenly I stare, dizziness brushing at the corners. With haughty sneers the guards slide off the handcuffs.

The great metal beast bares his sloping tongue. *I love you*, Alden mouths unmistakably. There is only darkness inside, another door. And when the shining circular portal slams shut, my best friend is gone. In his place is a quivering echo. A blunt thud. Now I know how my mother felt. That door . . . how can it not be death?

Sobbing tears burst through me, they shove me to my knees. All I can do is shake my head. Again and again. It's my fault. It's my fault. It's all my fault.

"Sempra?" Timothy appears behind me, stroking my fallen, rounded back.

His tender tone stirs the memory of the tallest building. Who knew of the book? Who else knew? Just me, Alden, my mom, and . . . and him. I pounce with the tightness of a lifetime's unexpressed rage. Blind action guides my fists to his chest.

"Wait, wait, wait," he takes a step backward, genuinely laughing. "Don't you get it? I *saved* you, Sempra. God. You should be *thanking* me."

Timothy stops my next punch before it hits him. He swathes my hand in both of his.

"They were gonna kick you out too. I was the one who convinced them that you hardly had anything to do with it."

"What the hell are you talking about?" My dry words tremble. The draining masses behind us disappear.

"Some guy across the street saw you one day," he bites his lip. "He saw you and your mom through the window, holding up a book. When he told the government, they were really freaked out. They thought maybe there was some . . . secret uprising being staged, or something.

"They knew you wouldn't tell them who else was in on it if you knew you were gonna get kicked out anyways. So they called me in to gain your trust. Find things out, you know."

He blinks without re-opening his eyes. A stray, green-stained hair bounces off his nose and drifts to the ground. I feel only a steady numbness.

"But . . . oh man, Sempra. I really did like you. It wasn't an act, like it was supposed to be. I couldn't do it. I just kept stalling time. Alden was an easy guess, right from the start. But I kept putting it off. Then they started to pressure me. They started threatening to kick me out. I had to do *something*.

"So I found out for sure that it was Alden who you got the book from. And I just.. I told them that you found the book on the street and were about to turn it in, when Alden stole it from you, claiming it was his. You didn't tell anyone after that because you didn't think they'd believe you. That was the story. And they bought it, Sempra. They bought it. I did all of that for *you*. I saved you. Because . . . that's what people *do* when they love each other."

Pure, aching silence. It drums against my ears. Timothy looks slowly down at me, expecting me to hit him or to kiss him. I choose neither.

"Why did you do any of it in the first place?" I squint into his tarnished face.

"Well, they came into my old class," he shrugs his shoulders up.

"They offered me money for the job 'cause they thought you'd like me . . . they thought I'd be willing . . . I wasn't born rich, Sempra."

When my fingers smack his face I think I'll go deaf. Passively, I wring out my throbbing hand. A yellow mark is left on his cheek.

"How could you do this to me?" I say with my hollow eyes more than my mouth. Already I'm creeping away from him, this hideous traitor. One foot shuffles backward, then the other. The soles of my shoes are smooth against the gray, stifled pavement.

"Sempra," Timothy calls out. But now I am running again.

Past cloned buildings that observe us tiny people, that giggle at us with hatred. They are just as much as us, aren't they. We are no better.

Only after Timothy is miles behind me do I slow to a jog. Memories itch in long strings against my body. If I keep going there are walls in the way. I want to curl up and just stop, stop everything, ignore this surreal, orange world. All I can do is go back home.

Our apartment offers no comfort. Nothing can comfort one who won't see, who has nothing left but regret. Nor is there relief in my mother's soft arms cradling my head.

"There was nothing you could have done," she kisses my forehead. "It wasn't your fault."

That morning I lie awake, eyes to the window, unable to think of anything but how very wrong she is.

FOUR YEARS LATER

CHAPTER THIRTEEN

What are we doing, if not waiting to die?

Our nights are bright like ancient days once were. A synthetic sun never truly sets. Night is day, while day is day. There is no night anymore. We are rows of heavy boxes, soaked always in warmth-less light. Night killers.

All for staying and working. Stale time spent in breathless, angered stupors. Broken people who can only smile when the other's backs are turned. Always chasing after it. Searching for simplicity's modern touch.

Metal and plastic bind us, not to this world, but to the idea of it. And I have to wonder—are our false idols even worthy of such worship?

This is what the others call life, but I'm not so sure.

I've tried. Tried to do it their way. After fourteen grades, school is over. These past few years my mother has kept a steady hand on my arm, urging me to keep my eyes closed. To ignore. To forget.

"Just get through it, then you can come work with me at the clothing dispensary," she says with chocolate brown hair, then with graying fronds behind the ears.

So I went to class bathed in a four year silence. Natalia was the only one who lowered her gaze for Alden's absence. Maybe we would've become friends, if I'd had room in my mind for one.

In my solitude, I read whatever pre-facility e-books I could find. There weren't many. I suppose the government allows a few to satisfy the minds of the inquisitive. Television works well enough to distract the rest.

"You should spend some more time with your friends," my mom often advises, leaning against the doorframe as I read. "Whatever happened to that Timothy boy?"

Timothy was moved back to the non-accelerated class. I hoped with all my being that I wouldn't have to talk to him again. Then one night he followed me home. Silhouetted against the chrome cove of the train, he told me he loved me, he was sorry. It was only he and I, rocking back and forth in time with muted train rhythms. How it hurt to know that he was truthful, but wrong. I couldn't ignore him anymore. His voice rose to a whimper. All his imperfections suddenly stood out, giant forehead and sunken eyes.

"You don't love me," I spat, finally looking at Timothy. "If you did, Alden would still be here."

His face then was shocked into still, dark water. He stayed there, a ghost, even when I got off. And I haven't seen him since.

Mom doesn't know about any of it. She only knows that Alden is gone. Sometimes it's all I know, too.

That door has opened and closed for me many times. Always I wonder why I don't follow him. Fear that they are right? Or worse, that I am wrong?

For years I have been a statue while everyone else shuffles around me. My life here isn't going to change. Not while everything I lack is waiting on the other side. What I have to do is change it myself.

As I gather my things into a pillowcase, for we have no bags, the facility seems to shrink. It holds no power over me. Not anymore. I roll up two extra sets of tunics and trousers, white as always. Underclothes. My frayed toothbrush and a toothpaste tube. Soap for body and face. When I come to the brown, plastic comb lying on the bathroom counter, I hesitate. What will my mom use, if I take our only comb? As I walk away from it, it too begins to shrink.

In the dim kitchen I find a few flavors of mush, unopened in their packages. A handful of vitamin D pills. I fill an empty jar with water. Screw the lid on tight. What else? What else?

With widening eyes I remember the night the heater stopped working. After adding a thin blanket, the pillowcase sits lumpy and full, propped up against the wall.

Mom will be home from work soon. I'm supposed to start my job with her tomorrow. Arm in arm, wearing matching polyester work suits. Hours of *this is my daughter, Sempra.* Polite smiles, ramblings of *oh yes, I see the resemblance.*

Instead I'll be sneaking away before she wakes up, hoping the sun sets by the time I reach the outside. Saying goodbye would be impossible. She'd just try to stop me. And she's the only reason I would ever consider staying.

Wetness garnishes the purple skin beneath my eyes. Wouldn't it be easy to crawl back into a warm bed, have a snack, watch some TV? To forget all and everything? But that's what I've been trying to do for four years. And it hasn't worked.

When she comes home we eat dinner. I keep going over everything in my head, the last this, the last that. Mom asks why I'm so quiet. Shrugging, I swallow my last bite of bread-mush.

How can I leave her? Her tired, bony arms? Her kind, soft voice? She'll glimpse in at my empty, rumpled sheets and know. *My daughter is never coming back.* Hovering in my room for hours, unblinking, she'll forget about work. Finally her boss will call her and she'll say she's sick. Then, sitting on my bed, the tears will come. They'll never end, not really. Both her husband and her daughter. Gone...*dead.*

I can't sleep but I pretend to. Shivering with nervous dread, I count the threads of the off-white curtain that I've kept closed for four years. It's a protector, hiding me from the faceless man across the street.

In the forced darkness I stretch my arms timidly. I leave my phone on my nightstand, walking away, for the first time, without it. Sling the clunky, rattling pillowcase over my shoulder. This is it. One hand rests on the front door.

"Sempra?" My mother snaps on the light, squinting through its brightness.

If the pillowcase didn't declare my plan aloud to the world I would run back to my bed. Mom swallows heavily.

"You weren't even going to say goodbye." There's no question behind it.

With a sigh I drop the bag to the floor. My gaze follows it.

"I sent you a text for when you wake up. I knew you wouldn't want me to leave." With each word I want to say *I'm sorry* instead.

"You're an adult now, you can make your own decisions," she holds her head up. "I always knew this would happen..."

The strength melts away with her voice. She crosses her arms, clothed only in silky white pajamas. We're silent for a moment. The clock drums louder than it ever has before.

"Why don't you come with me, Mom?"

"Your father told me he'd come back for me if he could," she narrows her eyes. "And he didn't. He didn't. He's not here. What does that tell you, Sempra? That he doesn't love me or that he's dead. Either way, there's no reason to—"

"Maybe he can't reach you. Maybe . . . maybe he's camped right outside the door, waiting for you."

"I guess you'll find out, won't you."

Suddenly the doorknob is turning beneath my fingers without me even realizing it. Slipping, skin on smooth metal.

"I love you, Mom."

She grabs me around the shoulders. We hug each other. My nose digs into her neck. I blink away tears.

"I love you too, Sempra."

Then I balance the pillowcase against my hip, and step away from first, from only.

I ride the train as close as I can. It takes another hour to walk the rest of the way. All I can see are gray, blurry outlines. The lights are just blushing red when the door emerges, striking and bronze, from the wall. Alden's face turns to me, calmly mouthing *I love you,* once again. One guard stands haughtily in front of it.

He eyes my pillowcase, creasing his flat, sculpted nose.

"You want out?" The guard chuckles, nodding to the door.

"Yes," my voice rings clean and crisp.

Furrowing his thick eyebrows, he leans jokingly toward the handle.

"You sure?" He smiles viciously.

Silently, I shift forward. The guard pulls a slim key out of his pocket, thrusting it into the door. It creaks. He stares at me with wide eyes. I hold my breath. What I'm doing has never been done before. Is it even allowed, I feel him wonder?

The lights jump up one level, yellower by the minute. People will start leaving for work soon. What a spectacle this would be.

"Do you really know what you're doing? You know what's out there, right?"

"Yes," I nod. Alden and my father.

So he opens the door. I walk into the dark room inside. The door slams bluntly behind me. It sounds different this time. Not like death. No, more like panic. Blindness squeezes my vision. Desperately, I feel the walls of the metal room for the outer door. Already the air is thinner. Colder.

Finally I shove open the immense gate to the outside. And, as a strange pale light shines on my arms, I become the first person to leave the facility of their own free will.

CHAPTER FOURTEEN

The sky folds and unfolds in a dizzying fabric. Pins of light dart from ever-increasing blackness. It's like the air moves in strokes of paint, saturating the dusk earth with waves of dark purple. Rich, velvet hills coat the distance. Above them drip woven clouds of pink.

Such intense enormity I have never seen. Only steps outside of an old world I stand, fascinated with the glowing white face of the moon, so sparsely speckled with lakes of shadow. This ground beneath me is light brown dust, already claiming the edges of my shoes.

All at once flies at me. Clean, wide. Endless stretches of low, blue shrubs nestled between whistling bundles of grass. Facing the distant hills, a grove of thick-trunked trees. Trees. And every few minutes, a sweeping rush of air. Everything sways with it. I can see why, the way it embraces you, smelling of chill and of warmth.

Our textbooks explained the world with stale words and dull pictures. All of this is familiar, dirt and plants and moon. But now I know—nothing can really show you the wind. Not until you feel it brush past your own outstretched arms.

It's cold, but I'm not yet shivering. Opposite the hills I see some sort of a structure. The sun has set, but it will probably come back again soon. When it does, I'll need somewhere to hide. Taking a deep breath, I start humbly toward it. The pillowcase is already starting to grow heavy.

So this is the world. There are no festering piles of corpses. No savage outsiders. At least, not yet. All I see is beauty and air and sky. What more is there to discover? Lakes, rivers? The last survivors of snarling, wild creatures?

With my head dropped back to watch the moon, I stumble towards the crumbling shack. As I get closer, I see it's made of splintering boards of wood. The roof points upward in a triangle. On one side there's a rectangular opening. No door. A window with jagged glass teeth protrudes from another wall. It's obviously an ancient dwelling. Who would live in such a place now, with all that light spilling in? But it's better than nothing, I guess.

I climb two moldy stairs, then peek inside the doorway. Only now does it occur to me that someone else might already have claimed this spot. Moonlight reveals nothing but an empty, dirty room.

Inside, it smells like the book. Old, stuffy. The pillowcase slides out of my hand. Dust consumes it, instantly and heartily. I sit cross-legged on the filthy floor. My eyes adjust. In the corner, a mountain of spider webs wave though no wind touches them. Dirt settles in sticky gloves over my fingers.

How long will it take for the sun to rise? If I keep going, it might come up when I have no protection. Better to wait out the day, so I have a whole night to begin my travels.

And then what? Desert horizons extend on forever. You can't just follow streets or silver walls. In this endless landscape, Alden could be anywhere. And my father could be anywhere else. They could be on opposite sides of the planet. That is, if they're even alive at all.

Though I thought it impossible, the heavens have fallen even blacker. A chill forces its way down my shoulders. Arm hairs stand up between small, round bumps. I'm shivering so roughly that it hurts. Suck in breath, push it out, through tingling teeth. Curling up in a ball, I unfold the blanket. Wrap it around me. Thank you. It helps a little. Just a little.

Hours pass, and still it is sunless. After falling unsteadily asleep, one corner of the sky is pale blue. How can it be so unbearably, unrelentingly cold? Suppressed regret spills around me. Look at me here, shaking in a half-collapsed hut pierced with gaping holes.

A bed. Think of plush warmness. Cushions, mountains of comforters. Sitting down to a never-ending supply of food. All of that is gone. Gone forever. While this world holds wonder, it does not hold comfort. One must be exchanged for the other.

Finally, true sleep overcomes me.

Then a light is soaking the inside of my eyelids in scarlet. I wake up. The sun beams through the broken window, right into my face. It doesn't burn like I imagined. But still I cower away, crawling to the center of the room. Away from all openings.

Through the doorway I can see the facility. Nothing but a small black dome, lost in a land of giants. Suddenly I feel even smaller, having once thought such a place immense.

Sunlight dresses the plants in brighter hues. And the sky. I don't think I'll ever tire of it. What a magnificent blue, no clouds at all.

While I sit and wait for the sun demon to leave, all I can do is eat or sleep, clammy with old sweat. Only once do I try to look into the sun's face. A fiery, white orb. It bites at my watering eyes. With this discovery, the sun is no longer a physical thing, but a feeling. More like the wind than the moon.

This star, our sun, was the only thing they never showed us. They let our imaginations mold him into a terrifying giant, instead.

Red finally replaces blue. Bands of warmth trace the hills as the crimson sun sinks behind them. From above, some animal cries. It's probably a bird, but I never see it.

When the only sound is silence, I stand onto weak legs. Dust off my tarnished pants. An indent in the doorframe catches my eye. It's a word, carved into the old, soft wood. Welcome. Each letter sits below the one before it. Simply falling. Who once crouched there, ripping away chunks with a dull knife? Perhaps it was the result of boredom, of hiding like me. These marks could be here until the end of time, couldn't they. And the ends of the Earth could be near.

I wilt down the stairs, the side of my ankles worn from rubbing against the floor. Stuffiness is wiped clean. Outside, everything is dynamic. The oppressiveness of grandiosity is cut away.

Every direction circles around me. Which way? To mountains, to grasslands, to the sun itself? Which way is the sea? Then a great gust of wind drums over my head. And I can hear it; a golden rustling in full tree branches.

"Do you know what a tree is?" Alden once asked me with young, earnest eyes.

At that point, I didn't. But Alden's mother whispered stories to him. And he passed them on to me. I never knew much of his family, only that they were poor. They lost their son. That never bothered me before.

After hearing of towers crowned with green bursts, my dreams sucked them in and claimed them as their own. When, a year later, I saw a tree's photograph . . . it didn't match. There wasn't enough texture to it. Not enough life.

Now there's a whole grove. An entire forest of life. When Alden had this same circle in front of him, which way did he choose?

I might as well be following his footsteps.

CHAPTER FIFTEEN

It's a distinct possibility that I am the only person in the world. Just me and distant tree branches. And the occasional yelping noise in the bushes. Elusive birds, again and again.

There's no such thing as time anymore. Either there is sun, or there isn't. From blue to sparkled black and back again. Maybe I should jump around and laugh. Maybe I should lunge to my stomach and weep. I don't know what to think. So I just keep walking.

The openness of everything is astounding. There, down the hill, is the facility. Beyond it, carpets of dry dirt. Worn buds of wildflowers atop cracked stems.

Where is the moon tonight? And yes, it's really night. Stars upon stars . . . some flickering in unsteady streams of blue and red. So many that there's hardly room between them.

Dusty, long noise follows me. Sound here is wider and, at its essence, quieter.

How hard it is to walk in perfect, straight lines when there is no path to follow. Taking big steps never seems to get me any closer. One eye is always scanning the horizon, waiting nervously for the slightest dash of light.

My throat grows tense and rubbery. I throw down the pillow-case, groping through its belly to find the jar of water. All this walking and my legs are heavy. Warm sweat touches my face, the tips of my nose and fingers flushed cold.

With tepid water still sloshing over my tongue, I continue. The jar is a quarter gone already. There are blisters where my shoe rubs against my heel. Each step holds pain. But I have to get to the trees. Have to get to the shade before the sun comes.

And within only hours, after the coldest air passes through, a sunrise blossoms behind my back. I notice it first on my hands. Pink reflections. All I can do is run.

The trees have never seemed farther. Hot breath falls out of my mouth. My legs pound, not because I tell them to, but because they must.

Just as the head of the sky swells to red, thin needles brush past my shoulders. It's shaded now, but I keep running anyway. Green . . . green is above me. Slippery, stark and brilliant. Rows of columns with feathered plants at their feet. When my breath comes in, it's wetter and sweeter.

Then a heavy pressure knocks me down. The pillowcase explodes open, scattering its possessions among browning leaves. Lifting myself up, a twig digs into my palm.

Out of dense foliage springs a dark face. Smooth, long hair, rumpled on the side that hit the ground. A sleeveless dress in matte fabric. And, below spacious eyes, the plump cheeks of a child.

"Sorrywhatwereyourunningfrom?" Words fly quickly from her jumping voice.

For a moment I just stare. The girl shifts to her knees and crouches low. She's not wearing shoes.

"The sun," I finally gasp.

"Why?" She laughs, stirring tiny grey wings from the tree branch above us. "It'snotevenmid-dayyet!"

I stand up, brushing soil off my knees. A seriousness comes over her as she studies my outfit.

"Whereareyoufrom?" Her eyebrows furrow.

"The Circadia Stable Living Facility."

Smoothing away the forest's blanket of debris, I search for my pillowcase's lost fodder. An outsider. Trees. The forest. Pausing, I catch my breath.

"Neverheardofit," the girl shrugs.

When I find my water jar, I tilt back my neck to gulp it down. Only too late do I realize that it's empty. There's a crack in the bottom corner. From its lips fall the last drop.

"Isthatallofyourwater?" She skips over to me. "Icangetyoumoreifyouwant."

"The jar is broken."

The girl sticks her pinky finger over the hole.

"Wehavemore.Comeon."

Through the legs of giants we walk. How does this child know where to go, which way to turn? Gripping her swinging black hair with my gaze, I ignore the forest. This little ghost could be leading me to snarling death. Or to Alden. There is only her.

She leaps with the grace of a grown woman, one foot always warmly stroking the soft earth. Her arms float freely to the side. They brush away spider webs, dancing in a weightless manner I've never seen.

Spheres of light pierce softly through the canopy. Each one is wider than the last, until forest melts to a clearing. A meadow. Yellow, white, purple flowers wink from creaking grass. Round houses made of wood stand in a circle. And, in the middle of it all, a crowd of outsiders glare curiously.

"Who'sthis?" A curvy, middle-aged woman with wild blonde waves steps forward. Her voice is kind and strict.

"Iranintoher.Sheneedssomewater,Mommy," the girl, almost as tall as the woman, runs to hug her. "Shesaysshe'sfromtheserpentliv ingfacilityorsomething."

Why do they all talk so fast? As they look me over, I do the same to them. They wear dresses and tunics, molded from cloth or even animal skin. Some of the men are shirtless. All of them are dark, twice as brown as Alden. Their features hold the weight that comes from being mixed. Like all of us.

But their bodies look different; toned, taller. Some of them have braided ropes tied around their wrists or ankles. One of the older women wears sticks in her ears. Earrings. None of them have shoes.

How can they smile, parading out there in the deadly sun? I wait at the edge of the shade. The blonde woman comes toward me with her head tilted.

"Soyou'refromsomesortoffacility?Where'sthat?" She stands next to me.

"Right down the hill, over there," I lift my trembling finger to point to it, but all I see is a wall of branches.

"Oh," she straightens her back. "You're from the bubble. Josh!Josh!She'sfromthebubble!"

One of the shirtless men jogs over to us. His scalp is balding, but on his chin dangles a scrawny beard.

"Wehaven'thadoneofyoucomearoundforalongtime," he nods.

"Josh, slow down a bit. Remember that last man who came by? He could hardly understand us," the woman smiles down at me with tarnished teeth.

They both watch my lips, expecting me to say something. The crowd has turned its attention away from us already.

"I'm . . . looking for some people. Did a boy come by here about four years ago? Kind of small, scrawny?"

"Mmm," Josh taps his chin. "Idon'tthinkso. Hard to say. We never stay in one place for long."

I sigh hoarsely. Suddenly I can't help feeling very tired. A wind pushes a sharp gray cloud towards us. It smells heavy.

"But I'd tell you to go north. Most people live up that way, 'cause the land's still good and all," he adds.

I imagine myself trying to find north. Wandering for years, all the while a weary stranger. Me and my pillowcase trying and hoping. Falling to my knees in desert wind.

"You can stay with us as long as you like, sweetie," the woman lays a hand on my shoulder. Her fingernails are caked with dirt. "We'll get you some more water, too, don't you worry. I'm Claire, by the way. This is my husband, Josh. And you already met my oldest daughter, Mani."

"I'm Sempra."

They start back toward the village, Mani running ahead. How can they do that? Won't they be zapped with rays of radiation springing from the sky? Don't they know about the sun's menacing strength?

"Youcomin'?" Josh laughs. "You look half scared to death. Don't worry, we don't bite."

"No, it's . . . it's just . . . what about the sun?"

"What about it?" He laughs even more, deeply and wisely, shaking his head. "As long as you cover up a bit out in the desert, and stay in the shade around midday, it's no problem."

What? . . . What?!? This . . . this doesn't make any sense. But here they are, brown skin immersed in direct sunlight. Shouldn't they know, more than anyone, how things really are? My whole world, my whole life, has just been ripped apart. Maybe the ozone layer has gotten stronger since they've made the facilities. Or . . . the sun has grown weaker. Or they lied to us. Probably the latter.

We stride back to the meadow's center. I stay cautiously at their heels, clutching my pillowcase against my chest. As the sun hits my face, I hold my breath.

Women stand chatting around a ring of stones. Above it is some sort of wooden rack. And inside—a child of the sun. It ripples like thin fabric, cursing and swaying. Hot air pushes off in red beads. That same smell from earlier comes from this creature, flying away in silver venom.

Living or not, he stares at me, speaking in ancient, watery whispers. The textbooks failed to mention this thing. I have no name for it. Whatever it is, it's impossible to look away.

Claire introduces me to the women, who wave with their fingers extended broadly. She explains that the others are out fishing. Why, I want to ask. But she's already nudging me gently towards the trees. In her hand is a metal bowl. Something familiar.

Within the forest, air beats along the soil in cold pulses. A delicate, round song that has long clung to the trees finally escapes into entirety. Two sandy steps away flows free water.

"We'll boil this for you," Claire raises her voice over shrill birds, over the water's drumming. "Don't want you to get sick, now."

As she swiftly kneels, letting the bucket catch the stream, I look up. And, oh, how tall they are. These trees that scoop sunlight into their leaves. Deep, plumed beings. Everything here is old, so old.

Shouts echo from farther down the stream. Water drops slide down the bucket as we walk back.

She hangs the water on a hook below the wooden rack. The yellow beast licks at it, yelling in blunt pops.

"What is that going to do?" I ask. None of this makes any sense.

"Well, you know, the kids just sip right out of the stream half the time, but they've built up a tolerance to it. When you're not used to the germs, it's really better to disinfect. My aunt could never handle it, she always boiled hers. Every day. Course, she was a pretty sickly woman."

"So that's what this . . . thing is for?" I'm embarrassed to have to motion to the sun child. It seems such a central part of their world. Almost like a deity. Of course I should know about it.

Her amber eyes blink slowly.

"What, the fire?" Claire opens her mouth, looking sadly down at me. Like she finally gets it. "The last guy like you had been around for awhile. He'd already figured things out. But you . . . you're fresh from the bubble, aren't you? You haven't even seen half of this stuff before."

Fire . . . so that was what they were talking about in *The Call of the Wild,* that substance that gave warmth and made no sense. Here it is, come to life. I mean to reply, but instead I yawn. My head is throbbing with tiredness. She smiles again at me, close-lipped.

"Come on, you can take a nap, if you like."

Claire brushes a wavy lock out of her face, leading me to one of the huts. In the middle is another circle of stones with black blocks in the middle. A hole dangles in the roof above it. Around the walls are scattered blankets and cushions.

"You can sleep here for now," she smooths one of them. "I think Rythe has some extras . . . I'll ask her later."

After so much, so much everything, I set down my pillowcase. Sitting on the hard ground, I feel a sudden loneliness. A rush of loss. And, more than anything, I miss my mother.

"Isn't everyone else going to go to sleep soon, too?"

"What?" She answers, grinning. "No, sweetie. The day's only just begun."

CHAPTER SIXTEEN

Waking up is a lot like going to sleep. That's when all the thoughts come. Looking around this circular room, warm and smelling like grass, my first thought is of where. Then outsiders, forest, fire, stream—they all come rushing back. And I slide out of the musty blanket, place my feet on the dirt floor. What have I done, what have I done.

My mouth tastes sour, so I dig out my toothbrush. Squatting in the corner, I clean my teeth. There is a cloudy puddle against the wall where I spit.

Outside, the sun is paler. Still, it cuts streaks against the meadow. Within the forest, night begins to stir.

"Look," screams a hairless toddler. "It'sthebubblegirl!"

A hundred eyes pass over the fire and cling to me. Black, brown, gray framed faces narrow questioningly.

I'm not from a bubble, I want to say to this ignorant child. All of them look wild and unkempt. The sun child paints their chins orange. *What do any of you know about anything at all?*

Atop the wooden rack, four pinkish squares sizzle. Even from the hut I could smell their humid aroma.

Mani floats away from the pack.

"Sempra," she squints up at me, for I'm evidently her personal responsibility. "Areyouhungry?Doyouwantsomefish?"

Fish? Is that what they're displaying on that wooden pedestal?

"Is it . . . dead?" My mouth droops open.

She nods, half smiling. With horror I contemplate the roasting carnage. Neither dead nor alive have I seen a fish. They must be heating it up, like an archaic microwave. Textbook illustrations of starving ancients stabbing helpless creatures come to mind. Bearded men prodding spears into bushes. No one has to do that anymore. Not in the facility. But here, they still do it anyway.

"Sempra! Come have something to eat," Claire waves me over.

We sit cross-legged on the grass along with the others. A teenage girl with a wide nose scoots over to make room. On her other side is a boy with shoulder length hair. Both of them nibble chunks of fish straight from their fingertips. A wrinkled man hands me and Mani our own white slabs, resting on leaves.

"Put some of this on it," Claire reaches into a clay bowl, sprinkling its contents onto our fish.

"Raspberriesandmint," Mani explains. She pinches off a piece, chewing it eagerly.

This doesn't look like food. The idea that this is dead, dead flesh, is absolutely repulsive.

"What's wrong?" Claire glances at my untouched meal.

"I'm just not used to this kind of food," I watch the fire. "I'm not used to eating things that used to be alive."

The old man who served us our fish turns from the fire. He crosses his arms, his cheeks sucked in sternly.

"Everything we eat has once been living," he slowly, defensively, begins. "All plants, all animals, all fish, were once alive. This is the way. Death is an unavoidable part of the natural cycle; for us, for all creatures. We give our respect to those who die so that we may live."

Everyone is quietly chewing. A bird whistles from the forest. Josh clears his throat timidly.

"What is it that you ate back at the bubble?" He asks me.

What was it, I think? What was our beloved mush? Did I ever really know what it was made out of? We had very little concern for food. It was an afterthought. A pleasantry.

"Vitamin-enriched synthetic fiber."

There is a silence. The old man nods gravely.

"And where did it come from," he tilts his eyes to the horizon.

"A factory, I guess."

Again, the soundless sighs. One woman coughs, throwing spit over the meadow. By now the clouds are heavy with deep blue.

"So this is what you prefer, then. Something that comes, not from the earth, but from the hands of man," the wrinkled man inhales, his stomach clutching in to his ribs.

"Douglas," a worn, freckled woman shouts. "Comeeatsomefish !It'sgettingcold."

She holds out a serving of fish covered in red sauce, her wrists shaking slightly. The old man steps roughly over to her. Mani glares hastily at my untouched plate. I imagine it tasting like metallic blood, coating my tongue in thick slime. Josh throws two more freshly cleaned fish onto the fire.

Behind the crowd, the young select dead fish from a swollen basket. They slice open scaled bellies with a knife. With their fingers, they caress the plush organs into another basket. This one is even fuller than the first. It stinks of urine, of yellow. The fish are sliced in half, then handed off to be cooked. Catches. Triumphs. Prey.

Join the savages, I can imagine Ms. Morgan saying. *What filthy barbarians!* This is all I can hear as I take a bite. Wet, graying squeaks of un-living flesh. And then I push it against my cheeks. Flaky, soft texture. Sweet, papery tastes. So I take another bite. Then another.

"Good, huh?" Claire smiles.

We eat until the basket is empty. The guts are taken out to the forest by three tall men before the sun hides away.

When I ask why they do this, Josh mentions bears, bobcats, cougars. Of these names, I only recognize bear. That could've been me, sleeping alone with killers. I relax my shoulders a little. At once I am glad for these people.

Stories are told of catching fish with spears, with a net. The young ones dance, the old stand with their backs to the fire. After words and words pour over me, they don't seem to come as fast.

Stars solidify out of what could be dust. Then the fire becomes dark red rocks, families start to wander to their huts. A cold that steals my own breath rolls in. Claire murmurs her goodnights and starts toward bed. Mani and I follow her.

Four more children burst in behind Josh. Three shaggy-haired boys and one whining girl. They fly in the dark to their blankets, snuggling contentedly in. Claire kneels before each of them, petting their foreheads.

Josh flicks sparks of fire into the circle of stones. A pile of severed tree limbs sits next to it. After hitting some sort of rock, a flame grows from twigs and grass. As it builds, he gently lies down more wood. Smoke dances to the ceiling, pooling in dusky clouds before shrinking away into the hole.

Next to Mani's bed is a new set of blankets. Light brown. Animal skin, they say. From a deer. This troubles me until I stroke its softness. I lie down, take off my shoes.

"Mani," I whisper, still watching her parents. "How many times have your parents been married?"

She rolls onto her stomach, sleepy eyes blinking.

"Just once, to each other," she chokes.

My eyes dart to each child. Each brother and sister.

"Oh," I reply, but her head is already covered in blankets.

Within the flickering shadows I see Claire and Josh hold each other, even in sleep. Her hand over his ear. His on her elbow.

As I listen to deep breathing, to snores, to fire songs, I let my mind free. And I think of how different we are. I'm always holding them at an arm's length. They were the ones who didn't make it to paradise. There are no televisions here. No cell phones. I can't trust them yet. Not completely.

It's hard to fall asleep. This is when I usually wake up.

And then I think of stars, of the sun child. Wind and trees.

And then I realize, half awake, that maybe I don't know anything at all.

CHAPTER SEVENTEEN

Sunrise is the dry incense of vanished fires. The chilled mirrors of trees burnt black into the ground. Birds, like stars, appearing one by one. Then, all of a sudden, there they are. All of them. They were just hiding the whole time. That's all.

We emerge from dying warmth into ceaseless shades of blue. Meadow grass shines with sallow water. Whatever sunlit tendrils weave their way through the trees are stolen by these water droplets. Glistening. And we step on them, crunch. Flat-footed. Now it's ours, this wet skin up to our ankles.

Douglas, the old man from last night, kneels stiffly at the central fire pit. He coaxes flame from silver stone, before blowing fiercely beneath a pile of sticks. Then erupts sun child's brilliance. The old man stumbles to his feet. Stretches his back. How can they be used to it, this magic of something out of nowhere?

A short woman shuffles around to the growing group of yawning outsiders. Her smile bares a missing tooth as she offers berries from a wooden bowl. Large, red berries topped with leaves. I take only one. Biting off a chunk, I flavor it. It's sweet, splashing liquid. Mani is on her third already. She stares off into the woods, sitting on the damp grass with bare legs.

Besides this mingling, it's mostly families who stay together in groups. Claire, Josh, I, and their five children stand at a distance. They plan the day ahead. Food for them and food for the fire.

"We'll go with some of the other teenagers across the stream," Mani wipes her stained hands against the grass. "We can forage, and pick some berries!"

While I brush my teeth, the others chew the skin of trees to freshen their breath. When I ask about bathing, they say we'll go for a swim later. If I stand too close to some of them, a musty smell rises from their skin. But no one stinks, not really.

Everyone heads in their own direction, clustering here and there. The girl with the wide nose and the boy with the long hair join Mani and I as we stride away from camp. Everyone just calls them the twins.

"Isn't anyone else coming?" Mani asks over her shoulder, balancing two woven baskets on each hip.

"No, they're gonna fish again," the shirtless boy replies. His green eyes rest on me. "I'm Tithe, by the way."

"Oh, and I'm Ann," the girl breathes, barely a whisper. If there was any other noise besides water or wind her words would be lost.

"I'm Sempra," I nod. But they already know that. I'm the new kid. The stranger.

We walk beneath fluttering leaves, yellow blossoms. Water slips over smooth rocks. It looks soft, continuing on a path to near-eternity. The dirt fluffs in red hairs at my feet.

Vines lace through weeping plants, up bases of trees. There is a hollowness to the ground. With each step I sink in, and it pulls on me. Mani and Tithe run ahead, leaving fleeting marks in the grainy dust along the stream. Ann watches their footprints dissolve.

Across the water is draped a fallen log. The others skip across it, barely glancing down. I heave myself up, using my arms for balance. Below is movement . . . but I am still. Little dots inhabit the air, blinking as a million miniscule eyes. Insects, I recall. Flies.

After crawling halfway I slowly straighten. My legs tremble. My fingers clutch peeling bark. They call this a bridge, this dead tree. They stand eagerly on the other side, waving and yelling with strange smiles. I'm not high up, but this is too much. Clear, swirling smells. Rushing, heavy noise that is twice the wind.

First one foot. Almost there. Then the other slips off the edge. And I land, with a splash, in the cold. Cringing, I look to Mani. Her young eyes hold no panic. She just walks to the edge of the stream, holding out her hand. So I push myself over slippery rocks. Through liquid curtains. It takes forever, but I arrive, shivering, on the earth. Panting, I sit on a mossy mound.

"You might wanna take off your shoes," Tithe smugly addresses the top of my head. "They're soaked."

"I guess I don't need them, anyway," I pull at the dirty laces. "None of you do."

"Only when it's cold," Ann kindly says with closed eyes.

I abandon my shoes and socks in a pile to gather on the way back. Now there are sharp sticks on my skin. Sticky orange sap glues leaf skeletons to my heel. Vicious bug creatures writhe below me, long worms with thousands of legs. The only place I can look is straight down.

From across the forest come cracking, splintering calls. Suddenly I stop. In great, sweeping lunges the trees bend. Such music. Such majesty. This wind is different than that of the desert. It sings. Leaves become green-white waves. Warm, dancing.

Each tree . . . each tree, there are so many. All different. By top and by bottom and by sheer individuality.

Mani, Tithe, and Ann all pause, turning back to me. They look where I'm looking, up to the sky. But they don't seem to see it the same way. Ann stretches her arms out.

"I love the wind," she smiles at the trees. Perhaps she feels a wonder for it still.

"Are you sure they're alive?" I ask no one in particular. "The trees? They don't act anything like us, or like animals. Do they even think, do they . . . feel anything?"

For a moment we all hover there. Waiting for the next gust to pound through. Tithe shifts his weight, clears his throat. But it's Mani who speaks.

"It's a different kind of life. They breathe, they grow, they have energy. Even if that's all we know, isn't that enough? What makes us any more alive than them?"

She keeps walking. And we follow.

The sun strikes down hotter now. I quicken my pace as we hit the open space between shadows. Soon we come to a sprawling gap among hanging branches. There, berries climb in high, dense bushes. Veined leaves cloak dots of red fruit. Mani drops the baskets at our feet.

"I think I saw more miner's lettuce growing over by the old willow tree," she jumps away into the forest.

Tithe and Ann each grab a tall basket and tear berries away from green stems. This must be their job. Like workers at a dispensary. From the ground I watch them, resting my bruised feet. They pull at one berry and shake the whole bush. Pluck and toss, pluck and toss. Both sets of fingers constantly in motion.

"Sempera," Ann timidly tries out my name, "aren't you gonna help pick raspberries?"

She points to the extra baskets. Slowly, I stagger upward. Isn't this their job? Nothing makes much sense in this bright, busy place.

Liquid leaks from the first rubbery berry I grasp. With sticky fingers I release its deflated corpse into the container. Tithe raises his coarse eyebrows.

"How old are you, Sempra?" He asks, still working.

Ann turns her head curiously our way, her arms hidden inside the bush.

"Twenty," I manage while trying to work another raspberry free. "How old are you?"

"We're seventeen," they reply one after the other, widening their green eyes.

Our voices drift off, replaced only by flapping leaf noises. The twins leave their crude baskets on the ground, throwing in handfuls at a time. Theirs are heavy. Mine . . . mine is more brown than red.

"Mani's only thirteen," Ann says after awhile. "She acts a lot older than that, doesn't she?"

It occurs to me then, while Ann's mouth turns down, how little the two look alike. Tithe's face is long. Ann's is wide. Besides their eyes and dirt colored hair, there is no connection. One is air. The other, rock.

By the time Mani comes back, with long reeds slung over her shoulder and a mass of foliage in her arms, Ann and Tithe are adding their own contributions to my slowly growing basket.

Walking back to the camp, I stare emptily. My mind is vacant, hollowed by all of this. I'm dizzy. Filthy. All because of this place that never looks away from the sky. They saunter over a bridge. I crawl across a fallen log.

A woman with a round belly pokes the fire with a stick. It's quiet. Raspy, crumbling wood exhales at her touch. Mani and the twins set down their baskets. Glancing at my empty hands, I suddenly remember my shoes. Bleeding wet in the forest.

"It's okay," Mani tells me, "we can go back and get them whenever you need them."

With this she glances at my dark brown feet, dirt wedged up the nails. Just like hers. Like everyone's.

CHAPTER EIGHTEEN

I'm tired all day, because that's when I was taught to sleep. When night comes, the tiredness leaves. It leaves because I tell it to. Sleeping on a dirt floor is uncomfortable. But it's not that. I'm getting used to it. No . . . it's the dreams.

Mountains of broken tree trunks, doubled in half. Flashes of orange light from the sky. I'm running, always running. There's something behind me. It's chasing me, but I can't stop to look. Faster, faster. Any second they'll catch up, they'll bind their hands around my throat.

A deep voice pounds into the ground and makes it shake. Out of nowhere spreads a hole at my feet. It has no bottom. Even though it's growing wider, I know I have to get across it. My legs pounce into the air. But then I'm falling. The darkness swallows my feet, my stomach. Desperately, I grope at collapsing pebbles.

One last, panicked look at the sky. And staring down at me, crouching at the edge of the crevasse, I see who was chasing me. Alden. My Alden. So I pull him down with me, sharply, angrily. I do it without even touching him. He opens his mouth to calmly explain. But before the words inch out, purple shapes take us.

When I wake up I still feel an ache in my throat. So close, then to die. Why didn't I just look over my shoulder?

My mind has been in other places lately. On broken pieces of here and there. The still colors of morning forcing the stream to pall to gray. How birds bellow their alien chants loudest when the light is leaving.

I've been thinking it's time to move on. This is all just a transient kindness. But I'm afraid to go. Somehow I'm more afraid now than I was when I first left the facility. Everything has evened out. The space around me has stopped being quite so enormous.

Mani runs with her long black hair, and nothing is even chasing her. If I close my eyes I still see her there. We sit by the river, but to me she is always gliding through the forest. Brushing against leaves so tenderly that they must love her. Certainly she loves them.

The stream doesn't really go on forever. It flows down, emptying into a great river. This is where we swim. Or, at least where they swim. It barrels so wide across that even the tallest tree wouldn't stretch long enough. Water here is darker. Choppier. Mud curls into liquid snakes as I kick my way down the banks. I try not to step on them, but they follow me.

While the others jump in, startlingly naked, I let my arms dangle. They dive swiftly into deep blue. Wearing my fraying underclothes, I plunge down and stand back up as quickly as possible. The cold water cuts at me.

Shivering, I climb up to the shore. Mani, Ann, Tithe, and the other kids wipe water from their eyes. Their hair bundles in thick spikes. I don't think I'll ever learn to swim as they do. Blending with the river's currents. Becoming indistinguishable from it. Something so mysterious is terrifying. For now, it's enough to smell the heavy roundness of primeval tears.

In the reflection of the water I can see the clouds. It's like there are two skies. Bees hum in the bushes behind me. An ant pauses before my leg, then turns the other way. Though it's still morning, I cling to the shade of a curly-leafed tree.

From the foggy river, the others emerge. Tithe slaps his hand into the water, throwing it in my direction.

"What's wrong?" he teases. "Don't they have water where you come from?"

"Of course we do," I yell back, though we've talked about this many times. "But it comes out of silver tubes! And it turns hot and cold with only the flip of a switch!"

He snarls at me, water droplets hanging in his eyelashes. My gaze falls to clear sparks of sand while the three of them throw on their mottled, worn clothes. Ann huddles next to the tree trunk. She absently strokes its gouged bark. Her hand is just as brown, only slender with veins.

And then I think of Alden, all of a sudden. If only I could become a giant and tower over the land, peering down into villages until I found him. Deep in my chest it's always, constantly there. Like something is pushing and needs to be done with.

"That last man who came was afraid of the water, too," Mani lets the sunlight bounce onto her face.

"Do you . . . remember his name?" Why did I never think to ask before? Maybe it's not Alden. But it might be someone I know.

"Ummm . . . I think it was something weird, something like . . . Bradley?" She waits with an open mouth.

"*Kern?* Kern Bradley?"

"Yeah, that was it! The old guy with the long hair. Did you know 'im?"

Not really, not really. He was just the man who was kicked out for being different. For coming too close to changing things.

Everything comes, again. Oh, all at once. They lied to me. To all of us. Why should I trust anyone at all? Especially these outsiders here. Is there any possible way to know who really knows?

When Mani first saw me swallowing my pill, she gasped.

"What's that?"

"It's a Vitamin D pill. Everyone needs them."

She stared at me, then. With her eyebrows weighed down.

"*We* don't."

So I stopped taking them. No one ever told me why I needed to in the first place.

And I've tried to learn, to learn how life works here. I came from a world of concrete towers. That's what I always tell them when they ask what it's like in *the bubble*. Just a barren dome where nothing grows. That's what I tell myself when my eyes shine wet. Because of my mom. Her and Alden, I miss them. Yet here I am with neither.

After we're dry, the four of us climb the hill back to the camp. My mom's warm smell stays in my mind, her soft arms. The way she looked at me that last time. Like she would never see me again.

Josh and Claire sit in the dry grass in front of their hut. They tenderly hold metal sewing needles, a prized commodity that's passed around to whoever needs it. Their children are running circles around the village, parading flimsy twigs in the air.

Claire molds animal skin together using a wiry string. I think it's woven from bark. She bites her lip and bends her head closer to each stitch. A moment goes by that I'm just hovering over them, amazed. Josh smiles at me. He itches his chin, dotted with hair.

"Where did the needles come from?" I wonder aloud, kneeling next to them.

"From before," Josh draws out his words, almost singing.

Before always seems dark. It seems like no one had faces back then.

Sunlight rubs at my skin. How nervous it makes me, the way it tingles. I step away towards the forest, looking for Mani. A wind falls down from the wispy crowns of trees. Delicately, my eyelids stretch into a mouth-less smile.

A round nail taps on my shoulder. Douglas's wife stands behind me. Her sagging forehead is plucked upward, and her grimacing lips bear cracks. We nod to each other. She's never spoken directly to me before.

"We're going to the valley soon. The seasons are changing already, and the fish'll stop coming." Her yellowing eyes wait for a response. When I give none, she continues. "Claire and Josh can't keep providing for you. They don't have the heart to tell you, but I've got no problem with it. Don't you see how many kids they have? That alone's enough."

Another breeze moves my hair. I sigh along with it, pushing air into air.

"But there's always plenty of food, more than enough to go around," I glance toward them, toward each child.

"There's less in the winter. Especially when people take their share without giving anything back."

She's quiet. With such a grim visage, I don't dare to speak.

"Either you start helping out, or you go. We can't afford to have little miss guest sitting around anymore," she says, raspy-voiced.

"They asked me to stay. So . . . I really don't know what I did wrong," I fight, throwing my hands in the air. Not to stay, but to defend myself. "But if you want me to leave, I will."

Away from her I rush. Ignoring Josh and Claire, I burst into the hut. Three sacks of water have been waiting next to my pillowcase for weeks. Made from an animal, of course. Organs or something. Like everything in this barbaric, murderous place.

With my things over my shoulder, I point my nose to the dirt. Don't look around, I tell myself. It'll just make it harder to go. The sides of my vision blur.

They call after me but I won't hear them. I refuse. Sempra, they yell, Sempra, in their fast, unintelligent voices. Taking big steps, I pace over the meadow, to the trees. Away from the sun, away from his child. Then Mani is in my path. She stares at me, just stares forever.

"Sempra, at least take some food with you," Claire shoves a woven container into my hands. Josh blinks behind her, breathing heavily. Douglas and his wife, the whole village, watch from the corners.

Isn't this too much to take, I think. Isn't this the problem?

"Why did you ever help me at all?" I ask. "I'm just a stranger."

"We're all people, aren't we?" She softly replies.

I consider hugging them. But I only whisper my thanks. And instead, it's Mani who wraps her arms around *me*.

CHAPTER NINETEEN

There are patterns in the ground. Where animals have stepped, it would seem. Dry gray dirt holds memories like photographs. They don't have real photographs here. Just circles kneaded on top of each other. Clinking teeth, shoving pungent breath away from fangs. Even though I can't see them, it's hard to forget there are wild creatures in the bushes.

How to find north, I have no idea. Mani mentioned the sun as the giver of directions, but how can that be when it blinds my eyes with glowing dots? Look to something you cannot look at. Ha.

Though the air is open in the desert, and distance there is touchable, I stay beneath the trees. My feet stumble on crooked roots. Glass strings of spider webs cling to my eyebrows. But at least there is shade . . . shadow. And at least I got my shoes back. The skin of my feet was turning gaunt and cracked.

I have no plan, except to find some other people. People who have seen Alden or my father. It would be hard to describe my father to others. Nineteen years changes a person. He probably has a spongy white beard, and shivering, dark hands. Maybe he paints rocks with animal blood, raising them up as offerings to the sun. A true outsider by now, certainly.

An odd taste coats the wind. After hours without looking back, I finally do. Nothing there. Just trees I don't recognize and walls I don't understand. My shoulders crease down, toward the ground. Breathe in and smell . . . oh, that weird thickness. But I suppose anything is fragrant compared to scentless *white*.

The dead, brittle leaves snap beneath me. Seems the sun is rattling, or dripping. Everything shakes with fog. I rub my eyes. Have I walked into a cloud?

Vague smoke blows from the distance. Choking, bitter. In front of green is a field of dust. Shining black masses. Here, the forest is gone. Beaten logs whimper in weak piles. And stillness, such quiet, brushes from the exposed sky.

Far in the hills I see a stream of red. Licking branches away, it is a smothering curtain. It takes me a moment, but then I recognize it. Fire.

Who birthed this enormous flame? Can the sun grow his own children, spitting them from his lips?

Timidly, I wade into the crumbling ground. Did the trees scream when they were wrapped in fire? My eyes fall to the wispy pieces coating my shoes. I suppose trees must be alive. After all, only the living can die.

As the fire beast burns along the curved horizon, I creep over scattered carcasses. Heat jerks down from the sun. It pours over me. Even as I turn my head, it strikes my ears. My teeth clench into a grimace. This pushes me faster, lulling me into a skipping, frenzied jog.

With each plummeting footstep I sink into the supple liquid beneath. From this blackened landscape grows one tree. One browned survivor, with spines sticking from his face.

Down a slight incline and there is green again. I look back at the startled bleak world ready to blow away. At the curved body of the last giant. Windless. The last flower to touch that misty air.

Swallowing hard against a dry throat, I close my eyes. Just for a moment. Is that what you're supposed to do, just keep going? Mani would know. She would know from where the fire crawled. And she would know why the sight of it makes my arms weak from shaking. At the edge of death and life I want to curl up onto my knees. But I don't.

Ruts of off-colored clay scrape the earth. No water flows there. Only wind. Exhaling the perfumed smoke, I stomp down another hill. My throbbing legs lead me clumsily. Ferns drape over my shins. This is their world, not mine, I tell myself as leaves bloom over my head. As I sigh with anxious relief.

Soon there are bird songs again, and the quiet floats away. Hours of walking have left my forehead slick with sweat. Itchy, heavy. Everything is so weighted. Like inside it is drowning, wet mud.

Timothy would hate this, I suddenly realize. Though he has been banished from my thoughts for so long, I try to imagine him in this landscape. Away from the dark inner walls of the bubble. How he would cry, how he would yelp like a spoiled child. And, watery-eyed, he would shuffle backward with his hands over his ears. Really, it's impossible to imagine him here. Because here, he could not exist.

Finally I stop to rest in the lap of a tree with two trunks. Propping my pillowcase against the pillar of scars, I sit down. The ground feels coarse. A bug limps over my fingernail. But my eyes are so tired that I ignore it. And I let sleep close them.

When I wake up my neck aches. The dusk has masked all but a weak, sinking sunset. My chest tightens. A flurrying air creature darts in front of me. Not a bird. Something black that catches the wind. That spins with it. I lift myself up against the wooly tree.

Looking around dazedly, I almost yell. What do I do, what do I do? Here comes night's darkness. In boulders I see unnamed animals, crouching low. In fallen branches I see the spears of savage outsiders.

So I decide to keep walking. At least they'll have to chase after me.

It's not much different, walking at night. Only the heat slipping past me in rapid dilution. My sight adjusts to the silver forest. I have no idea if I'm even walking in a straight line. But if I dig my feet into the earth, I won't go anywhere at all.

There are no stars between the branches. What sky I see is nestled in beige night-clouds. Shivering, I cross my arms.

Sometime before morning I hear a crunch. Dry bushes being shoved away. Then a man's voice grumbles. Another replies, grunting. I stop, my white shoe dangling above a dead leaf. Their sound is dull and muted. Still I blink violently through the blackness, searching for their glowing eyes.

"Water's that way," one of them mutters. His deep voice floods closer to where I crouch, frozen.

"You sure there's any left, this time of year?" The other snorts. "Only got ourselves a few drops last time."

"There'd better be a few damn drops left," he clears his throat, "that alone'd..."

Suddenly their voices turn, footsteps dying away, as they wander deeper into the forest.

I can't help but sigh, wiping my clammy hands against my pants. Don't they know there's a whole stream, a whole river, a day's walk behind me? They seem so different from Claire and Josh. So . . . rough. Even just by the way they spoke. Good thing they didn't see me. They're not the kind of people I'm looking for.

Faces curl out of soft colors stroked from the sun. Each one beams down on only certain things. On sky blue hills still cut with fire. On tired, yellowing leaves. If I look up for too long I start to shrink.

My stomach begins to complain, so I eat some of the berries Claire gave me. They're sweet and plump. Contentedly, I pop them with my tongue.

Out of stillness and no birds, no birds at all, an explosive noise roars. I jump up from the log where I sat, rolling to the ground. The basket spills berries over the soil. As I lie there I watch them, mounds of pink shrouded in spindly blades of grass. What was...

Again it echoes through the tree branches. Boom, louder than anything I've ever heard. The wind seems to shake with the sheer weight of it. Two more times it shrieks. Staccato, one after the next.

When I peak my head up over the log, I see movement far in the distance. A wisp of waving, white veined leaves. Men's voices drizzle between blasts. The same two I heard last night. I sneak one last look toward them.

And there I see a hairy, muscular man, a silver rectangle in his hand, holding up a lump of fur. The sun turns to him. It lights amber curls in his mane. He smiles down at the red, sticky blood. Then I close my eyes. And I don't move until the birds start singing again.

What the animal was, I don't know. But its long, unmoving ears and motionless eyes told me it was dead. Not to mention the blood. The gun.

Terrified, I rise up. I've seen the dead before, but not death. It occurs to me that this might be normal. Killing animals. For the last few weeks I've slept in the smooth skin of perished creatures. Maybe I never saw them do it, but Claire and Josh's people obviously kill more than fish and plants. Swallowing roughly, I nod to myself. Everything's alright, I think. Just fine.

With a glance toward where the men last stood, I grab my pillowcase. Time to keep going.

CHAPTER TWENTY

Tree roots peek out from the dirt, blanketed with crumbling moss. Between their meandering arms is a metal can. Farther ahead lies crying, forgotten rust. This one is gigantic. Maybe from an ancient kitchen. Sitting there, it reminds me of an obese body lounging in the strained sunlight. From his mouth flows a trail of decay. A trail of infinite rusted artifacts, peeling in the breeze.

It's hard to remember that there used to be billions of people. Ms. Morgan told us that in the most crowded cities, everyone had to stand arm to arm. Coughing on each other . . . that's how they all got sick. Of course, I don't really believe this. Not anymore.

Most people left. They died, long ago. That's why moss is starting to grow over the broken slabs of glass. That's why I've wandered three days now without seeing anyone besides those men.

Sometimes I feel like I might go home. Back to the facility. But I can't. I'm here, in this impossibly empty world. I'm here forever. Me and the ghosts of the dead.

My feet take me beneath the arches of flowering trees, beside the shores of a rocky creek. Everything is farther and fuller than I could ever have known. I find myself humming along with the moving water. It's thin, shallow. Gauntly, it spreads and dances in sparkling waves.

A few of the lower bushes are withering. They're lost to the reaches of some vast, colorless disease.

As the sun travels through the sky, I think I've learned to feel its presence. Mani told me that the sun rises in the east and sets in the west. East is right, west is left, she claimed. North is ahead, south behind. So if I keep night's pink horizon in line with my left arm . . . if I hold my right along with the red morning . . . then I am walking north.

North to villages of strange people. North to the land that aches and breathes. The only side of the sky that the sun never touches.

My ankle brushes against a thick white rock. It turns over in the powdery sand near the stream. Something about it is so different. It's textured like smooth wood, but white like clouds. There's a hole in one side. I nudge it with my toe, digging its entirety from the earth. Then two more holes appear, over a row of serrated . . . teeth.

The pictures come back to me. Cartoon illustrations of human skeletons presented humbly over crude captions. Never did the textbooks mention, *this is what you'll look like when you die.*

Seconds go by as the hollow face stares. The lower half of the jaw is missing. A whole row of teeth. What was pure white only moments ago now looks putridly yellow. Out of the water rises a muddy stink, and I just imagine how the corpse decayed there. How surely their blood trickled into the creek.

Curiosity and terror mingle, just briefly. Then I run. With my pillowcase tucked under my arm. With my hair dangling over my nose. I let myself sweat, as I jump over the wasteland of rust.

And suddenly the trees start to thin. The grass stands taller. My feet are caught up, not in vines, but in crunchy, beige meadow grass. After weeks of tree shadows, I can see forever.

Brown hills above, quiet valley below. Not desert, anymore, but white fields of wildflowers. The occasional tree, with wide leaves that hide silver bellies. And grass with feathery bunches at the tip. When the wind blows, they bow down.

In this way I can see the wind. As I slow to an open-mouthed jog, I watch the warm wind flow from the afternoon sun. First I hear the forest shiver behind me. Then it flies over the valley, yawn-ing and sweet.

Down the hill is some sort of structure. I sit down to take a break, first, drinking water. It tastes sourer than usual. Wiping the drops off my chin, I scowl at the bloated stomach or bladder or whatever it is. My mush is almost gone. The berries were lost a few days back.

So I saunter clumsily down to the fields, hoping for people who will loan me food. Nice, friendly people who will tell me I'm going the right way. Bees dash across my sight. They land on delicate red petals. I watch where I step so I don't crush them.

As I come closer, the structure becomes a wooden house. There are no windows, only a gaping doorway. Out of this dark passage emerge two little faces. They curve their heads outward, into the sunlight. A little boy and a little girl. Dark circles are stamped under their pale eyes.

When they jump down into the grass, their stringy, melting hair swings. Both wear scraps of torn clothing. The boy's is caked with dried mud. Neither have shoes, only bloody toenails.

Even from a distance I can see the bones sticking out from their cheeks. Their skin seems thin enough to make them transparent.

All they do is stare at me. Neither attempt a smile. Only their stoic eyes, the eyes of a six, maybe seven year old. Hard, crusty eyes that have seen the depths of hunger.

I'm ashamed of the way they scare me. Never before have I known starvation. Why do I feel such a chill behind my back? My gaze jumps to the reddening hills. What am I supposed to say to them? Obviously they have no food. It seems too much even to ask directions. Because I have nothing for them.

A woman hobbles around from behind the house. Her face holds weight, somehow, compared to her exposed ribcage. She reaches up her hand in greeting. No words come from her gray, cracked lips. The kids cling to her frail rags.

My instincts, though weak from lack of use, tell me to help. Help these beasts. Help these hungry, demon outsiders! I hear Ms.

Morgan, in her shrill, forced voice. Oh, I want to yell, I can't! I can't or I will starve too. Here, I am susceptible to a world of deaths. And without my mush, I'm even more helpless than they are.

The three of them watch me wander back up the slope. Their eyes follow me, in my off-white clothes and once matching shoes. I offer only a returned greeting. A hand in the air.

This is what they told us outsiders would look like. Thin. Ragged. Dirty. They warned us of their thirst for more. The lengths they would go to to satiate their appetites. Yes, they told us. But they never told us they would be *children*.

And, suddenly, fear is the last thing I feel.

CHAPTER TWENTY-ONE

For another day I stomp among the valleys. I can smell myself, the raw musk. My skin feels tight. Constantly, I stroke my fingernails down my worn limbs, scratching at the dirt. All the streams have vanished. Meadows have sky, not water. With nowhere to bathe, I slink across the landscape, dragging a veil of dust. All I can do is brush my teeth, at the very least.

The sun is here, again. It was better in the forest, where leaves made wide drapes to shield my forehead. Now it's so hot. Even the wind is heavy with heat. Whenever I see a tree, with a massive gray trunk, and hairy, creaking branches, I rest beneath it.

There, I study my arms. Is that red, mixed with darkening brown? The sun will burn you, they always said. It will carve boils out of you. It will peel away your skin until you are just a twitching red muscle. Then whatever's left will grow into tumors, cancer. And you will die. The sun is a killer, children. That's why we live here...

But I know better now than to believe everything they said. I've been walking through pure strands of sunlight for weeks. And listen; breath still echoes from my mouth.

Walking, my eyes start to burn. Massaging my eyelids, I blame it on the little sleep I've had. Each night I travel, then nap for a few hours after the sunrise. Darkness is too terrifying to sit still in. It's one of those things that cut at you, that pull your hair.

Sometimes when I wake up, I forget where I am. How did the ceiling get so big, I wonder?

Along the eternal horizon there are no secrets. What I thought was a dead tree turns out to be a metal pole. Gigantic, even taller than the dome of the facility. Its head is circled by blades that chop the wind. I stare up at it, squinting.

Farther down the hills I see a few more, and a cluster of buildings. Even from here I recognize the black squares that envelope them; solar panels.

Dazedly, I hope the people in this village are more like Mani and less like . . . the others.

Fields begin to change. From wild grasses they shrink to round, leafy mounds. The dirt here is dark brown, stroked into fertile rows. It smells of fragrant, damp soil. Each strip guards its own breed of plant. Some have berries. Others, tall wispy clusters almost like grass.

Looking closely, I notice a rubber tube with holes in it. Water leaks out of it, into the stems of the plant where it's nestled. Though it's still early, the sun melts the water, pulling it away in a light mist. Within this fog, the sun itself paints half a circle.

After what seems like hours I find myself standing at the edge of a house. It seems to be made of wood, with a shining metal roof. Cautiously, I step in front of it. Clean, glass windows. A tightly shut door. Inside there are only shadows.

Voices grow louder as I pass more buildings. Peering past the edge of one, I find an open area. A grassy circle. It's crowded with people. They stand in front of tables cluttered with baskets. Everyone has something in their hands. Bowls carved of wood. Long strands of dead animal fur. Bundles of bright green plants.

Alden could be here. He could be here. Out of this mass of brown, wild haired outsiders, I choose an older man. He has deepset eyes and white, woven clothes. In two steps, I'm standing beside him. He looks like he knows something.

"Excuse me," I tap on his arm, "I was wondering if you could help me."

The man glances at me from the side of his eye. Sniffing, he shifts some orange cylinders higher in his grasp. I'm immediately aware of my filthiness, and regret it.

"I . . . I'm looking for someone," I continue. My throat stretches and throbs. "A boy, short, kind of scrawny, about twenty? I guess he's not a boy anymore, then. Um. His name is Alden."

"Never heard a name like that. Don't know 'im. You should ask someone from another village. In the meantime, how 'bout some carrots, eh?" He fluffs the green tops with his thick fingers.

My stomach curls with emptiness. When I reach for one, he pulls away sharply.

"I meant, how about you trade for one," he spits behind clenched teeth. "Shit. Isn't that what we all stand around here for? Where'd you come from, with manners like that?"

All the voices. All the faces. This wrenching cluster of strangers shudders in waves of flat noise. Part of me wishes for the quiet forest creek. Or even to be out in the meadows again, no longer surrounded by those who stare.

"The Circadia Stable Living Facility," I recite.

His eyes turn skyward. Then his mouth opens, just a crack.

"The Circadia Stable . . . the bubble."

It's as though something has pushed down on his face. Each feature hangs lower than before. Darker. Now I notice how blotchy his chin is, irritated by tiny black spikes. His thin lips fold over.

"You're one of them. I bet he sent you, didn't he? To grab some more followers to go claim all of your so-called rights over at that ridiculous bubble dome?"

"No, I—"

"Well, you listen to me. You tell that Kern what's-his-name to lock himself in there if he loves it so much. It'd do us all a huge favor to be able to trade every month without getting an earful about our goddamn qualities of life. From a *lunatic*!"

He stops yelling, spit dripping from his mouth. Everyone turns away. They pretend like they weren't watching. Along each face I see gathering sweat. The sun is at its highest already. I want to leave, but what about Alden? This is my best chance of finding him.

Swallowing over a dry throat, I step backward. My heel slides over someone's foot.

"Sorry," I mumble, unaware they'd been hovering so closely.

"It's okay. Hey, you know, we couldn't help overhearing," the woman laughs. She reminds me of a flower, tall and thin. "We think we can help you."

"We know Alden. He lives in our village, just north of here," the guy next to her, probably a few years older than me, jumps in.

I don't say anything. I can't. All that I've done. After the great distances my throbbing legs have carried me. It almost seems too easy. Here I was, imagining him on top of some cliff. At the edge of the Earth somewhere.

The woman is neither young nor old. Licking her lips, she throws a strand of dark red hair over her shoulder. Playfully, she squeezes the back of her companion's neck.

"My son and I would be happy to show you the way. We were just about to leave, anyway," she tilts her head and raises her eyebrows.

All I do is nod. We walk away from the crowd. The air starts to flow more crisply. As we emerge once again into the fields, I notice their empty hands. Of all those people, I think they're the only ones who carry nothing. Both of them wear pale textiles like the old man. Not animal skins.

Back in these meadowlands, I want to run. To skip around. To shout great thank-you's that would then float away into space. Maybe that's what it would be like to dance, really dance. It occurs to me that this is the opposite of the facility. This openness.

There are more rows of plants on this side of the village. Lines and lines of red, green, dark purple. We meander between them. The woman takes long strides. But the boy is only half her height. He walks next to me.

"Guess we better introduce ourselves. I'm Marvin. Marvin Colorado," he begins to smile, revealing teeth crowned in brown gunk. Quickly, he closes his mouth.

"You can call me Gala," the woman nods from her place ahead of us. I clear my throat.

"I'm Sempra."

For a few minutes, silence follows us. Marvin keeps glancing in my direction. His round eyes loom over a small nose. When I look back, he blinks away. He shakes his shoulder-length black hair. It shines proudly with grease.

As we distance ourselves from the village, a plume of motionless smoke bellows out of its center. Not the hapless, hungry fire of the forest. This has a strained presence, a purpose. A song. Through the dimming air I can almost hear it. Words from when the sun was young. And so, too, was man.

Above us, the sky recedes. It deepens. No clouds hide the dying sun. If I could choose any color from which the world is woven, it would be this. It would always be this. The blue between sunset and darkness.

A few birds whisper in the bushes. Besides them, it's quiet. Gala stops suddenly when we come to a curved, leafless tree. It has white sponges on its side.

"We'll stop here and make a fire for the night," she rips off a crumbling tree branch. Specks of rotting wood cling to her fingertips.

She and Marvin arrange the sticks into a pyramid. Beneath them, Gala adds a pile of gray, dead plants. I just stand there, listening to them crunch. From her pocket she pulls a rectangular stone. Now, thanks to Mani's people, I recognize it as the giver of fire.

Gala strikes at it, crouching low. It glows, but the orange sparks don't last. Again and again she tries. Her soft features burn red.

"Mom, why don't you just use the lighter?" Marvin sighs.

"'Cause I don't want to use up the fluid," she sits up, shaking out her hand. "You know that's only for emergencies."

Finally the sun child reaches upward. Soon it shakes and races, a million lives swollen into one being. We sit close to the flame. Breathing in the warmth, I tilt my head back to see the first stars being born.

"How's Alden been?" I eagerly ask the fire. "I haven't seen him for four years."

Marvin and Gala fold their chins down, glancing at each other.

"Oh, um. He's fine. He's, uh, been busy lately," Marvin tucks a wet lock of hair behind his ear.

"You've gotta be wondering why we came all this way to the trading village," Gala raises her husky voice, "just to return empty-handed. Well, look what we traded some old blankets for."

She once again searches through her pocket. When her hand unfolds, a small satchel sits in her palm. Tugging on the delicate string, she opens it.

"They're seeds," she looks at me expectedly, "from just about every crop you can imagine. We have, what, ten more of these pouches?"

By now the last of the blue has disappeared below the hills. I feel inside my pillowcase for my blanket. Bumps have clustered over my arms. I pull the fading rag tight over my shoulders.

Crops . . . agriculture . . . farming? They told us how it doesn't work. How there could never be enough for everyone. How nice, clean factories flow much smoother. This most recent, albeit archaic, practice of our ancestors died out only a few hundred years ago. At least, for some people.

"We've got lettuce, carrots, radishes, celery, artichokes. Now that's some trading right there," Marvin yawns.

"Trading?"

"Oh yeah, I forgot. You're from the bubble. Trading . . . it's uh, you know, you give me this, I give you that?"

"That doesn't make much sense. There's no money involved?" I quietly reply.

"Ha," he laughs. "No one's used money for a long, long time."

Gala throws more sticks into the light. She and her son stretch out over the bare ground. They wrap their arms around their chests. Yellow grass brushes against their noses.

None of us have eaten anything. I think of the final traces of mush in my pillowcase. But I don't have enough for them. So I leave it hidden, while my stomach turns.

Sleep comes easily to these strangers. Gala snorts, her eyelids twitching. Me, I watch the sky move. It washes over me in fine, cold lobes. I think of Alden, his black eyes caught in the universe up there . . .

Morning is sheltered by faint clouds. The mountainous hills glow orange at the tips. Where once was a living fire, now only black dust remains. It's a foggy morning. The wind smells of spiced smoke.

And here I stand. All alone beneath a dead, groaning tree. Without even a blanket around my shoulders.

CHAPTER TWENTY-TWO

Two foodless days burn my stomach. Up the hill I trek until I realize that this is where it ends. So I climb back down. Far, far ahead, I see an abandoned city. I recognize it right away. Just gray, broken concrete, amidst the thread of yellow flowers. Remnants of the old ways. Split, piled rocks. They spread out under the horizon. Above them, the air is tarnished with beads of dust. There might still be people there. But not Alden. He would never reach out towards such an ugly sight.

I turn away from it, and walk towards the sun. Even farther ahead there is something shining. Clear, so, so white. It must be water.

My hands fall silently in time with my step. The side of my thumb is still rough, still throbs from holding my pillowcase for too long. Now I curl my empty fingers in, so the wind doesn't touch them.

The pain of hunger has stopped being dull and comes in piercing stabs. If I looked in my throat, I think it would be bloody. When I swallow, it feels like gravel. Thick, sharp pebbles scraping into me.

Forcing spit over my tongue stopped working hours ago. My mouth cries for the rough skin of the water bag. For its stale scent. The sun reaches into my eyes. Again and again and again, until I can't take it anymore. I don't want it on me.

How . . . how could they do it? Leave me with nothing. Mislead me with false words and distractions. They know how new I am to this world. Mani knows which plants to eat. Those idiots, gripping their seed pouches, probably do too. But I don't. There is no way for me to get food. There is no way for me to keep warm at night.

For the first time since I left the facility, I feel that emptiness in my chest. Helplessness. And suddenly everything feels big again. Alden could be dead. My father could be bones in the earth. There's no guarantee that I'm going to live, either.

This place is full of thieves and guns. The facility is full of controlling liars. So where must I look, but the great, never-ending sky.

Grass shifts beneath my shoes, breaking with dryness. Around me, the air seems to move too fast. I can't seem to keep my eyes open. Each time their folds are drawn back to see, the doors slam shut. They fall and they cluster with eyelashes. Just like clouds. Just like the sound of water.

With only blinking sight I feel my way. Tired. So tired. My neck falls back above shaking shoulders. If anyone were here to see me right now, I would probably look completely crazy. Completely bizarre. Half sleep-walking across the deserted valley.

It doesn't really matter where I go, anymore. I just . . . it doesn't.

When I look into the world, for a moment, I see a line. A faint shape blossoming against the sky. Some horrendous, flowing breath. Smoke from fire. Fire from people. Not in the old city, but towards the water.

Then I straighten my back, and let my eyes take me to them.

Bushy trees hang low to the ground. One by one, leaves drop in the darkening air. The wind pulls river scents along. Shocks of wet warmth, hidden, rising.

As I drift closer to the water, there is mud on my shoes. Cold drafts blowing upward, inward, caress my cheeks and join the sky. When I look down, I see a wide footprint left behind. It curves, spouting human toes at the edge.

Several more lead me deeper among the trees. These trees are different than what I last saw in the forest. They're wider, leafier. Upon their bark, streaks are written in white ink. Bushes with hairy, pointed leaves rustle beneath them.

Some of them hold dark berries. They look so much like raspberries. I wrap my fingers around one, then pull away. Mani told me to be careful. Some of them are poisonous, she said. She gave the same warning to her little siblings, who loved to mash up berries and draw sweet pictures with their blood.

See, Timothy would say. First Alden, now this girl. When are you ever going to learn to think for yourself? Even when you're all alone, you need someone else to fill your head. His face would bear teeth, then, in a smile without warmth. How could I ever have thought I loved him? Even for a second?

But now I am here, and I've escaped.

The valley has disappeared, and the hills with it. A squirrel jumps between branches, it's tiny legs flailing. I watch it with my whole and entire existence. When it lands, the tree bends forward. Crashing, losing needles. Then it continues on its way. And the birds sing a little louder.

Above this are dark clouds. Almost purple. But I can't stop to look because I'm tired and I'm hungry, and I'm leaning back towards those berries. And then . . . there is an arm behind the tree. An arm and a head.

He peeks out his brown eyes, and walks slowly next to me.

"Who are you?" Asks the older man, wrinkles framing his mouth. Around his shoulder is a long, curved stick with a taut string.

"I'm . . . I'm looking for someone. My name is Sempra," I swallow hard over the pain in my throat.

His thin chest, below an animal skin tunic, doesn't rise. Suddenly a smile spreads out, etching even more lines on his face.

"Sempra. *You're* Sempra. You're Alden's Sempra, aren't you?"

I nod. Tears come to my eyes. They make my nose burn. But I don't let them fall. Not yet.

"He's been waiting for you, Sempra," the man almost shouts. "He's been telling us about you for years! Oh, she'll find me, he said. She'll come someday. 'Course we didn't believe him. But you came. My god, you actually came."

Then the man wipes his brow. A drop of water has fallen from the sky. More and more come, bouncing against the leaves. They land in my eyelashes. It sounds so different without a roof. Softer.

Through the rain, we walk toward the village. Finally, towards Alden.

We cross a dry ditch, where water once ran. Strands of mud begin to cry against the dryness. At its end is a small lake, pounding and lurching beneath the sky drops. It no longer shines in white, but in gray.

On the other side is a cluster of long huts. Covered deeply in leaves and dirt, half buried in the ground. And a waving sun child, vomiting smoke. Dying proudly in the rain. Beyond this, I see both fields and forest. Green and red and blue.

All of it echoes and wavers. Human noises, cluttering around beneath the low-hanging clouds. Shaking and burning and finally just falling over me. The rain begins to disappear, evaporating in thin wisps. Gone as quickly as it came.

For a moment I feel like this is fake. Like I'm in a blurry dream-world, stumbling over fallen stones. Then I see him.

A young man, taller than me. Taller than half the other men. With skin the color of dead leaves. With a full chest and dangling, structured arms. And eyes. Eyes as dark as any night, as any space between stars.

He runs to me. His features are more distinct, but still hold such sweet familiarity. In his smile is all of childhood. I wrap my arms around him. Different from that scrawny boy in my memory, but still him. Still Alden.

And, in the back of my mind I can't help but think that I will never have to be without him again.

CHAPTER TWENTY-THREE

"Can you believe we're walking out here in the sun?" I run my fingers through my smooth hair, freshly washed in the lake with the sap of some foaming root. Its soft scent flies away. "A few months ago I thought this was impossible."

"What happened, exactly? They didn't . . . did they kick you out?" Alden asks in his new, deep voice. In his faster, slipping language.

"No. I came to find you, all on my own. You and my father. He . . . I never told you, but he's not dead. He was kicked out the year I was born. For rebelling."

I look away from him, down at the plants that tease our ankles. The garden, they call it. Stuck in rows, like at the trading village. Mounds and castles shaped from sandy soil. Spiraling, fragrant leaves, soaked richly in color.

These they nurture. In turns, the people sprinkle rainwater caught in pots. And with their dirt-coated hands, they pluck away unwanted pests. Two women and a man kneel among vines. Always with their eyes to the lake.

"Sempra, I—"

"Is this where—" Our voices tangle. For a moment, Alden's mouth slips downward. Then he shakes his head.

"Go ahead," he touches my shoulder. Fleetingly, though not timidly.

"Oh. I was just going to ask if this is where you get all your food." I brush my palm over a tall cluster of white flowers. The sight of my arm surprises me. It's wrapped in thin, woven fabric, dyed a subtle red. The brightest color I've ever worn.

"No, we still hunt, and gather wild plants. Sometimes we fish, if the season's right," he looks up at the distant meadow hills. At the uneven walls of trees. Down towards the clear, shallow water. "It's weird. Sometimes I forget that I'm not from here."

How could he forget? How could he possibly erase those walls from his mind? Four years is not enough to replace an entire, sunless lifetime.

We find ourselves on thick sand. It sparkles against the low morning sunlight. In each grain are tears spit from the rolling edge of the water.

The lake speaks in thick, molding sentences. Bending and opening whistles from the sky. Finally, my shoulders can lose their tenseness. My eyes no longer ache. Nor does my throat burn. Still, my stomach refuses to be tamed into placidity.

"Have you . . . killed animals?" I steadily inhale the fresh, damp smells escaping from the ground.

"You have to, out here. It's the way life is."

This answer scares me, but I know it must be true. There's a pause. My mind turns to the whole world as we stumble along the shore. Alden keeps looking back every few seconds. To make sure I'm still here.

"Remember that one time, right after you found the book, when you thought the government might be lying to us about everything? You were right, Alden. They lied about every single thing I ever thought I knew. How does any of this make sense to you now?"

"Berea and . . . and some others explained it to me, back when I first came to them. She's the one who gave you that dress. I guess you could say she's the leader. Everyone goes to her for advice."

He leads me back toward the half-buried huts. Only a small hole peeks out from under the dense roof. If it weren't for that, or the wood supporting it, they would almost look like hills. Grassy, clothed in decaying plants. Inside is both blindness and warmth.

Most of the village has wandered away into the ancient forests, or to work quietly in the garden. Only a few elderly faces remain. One is Berea, squatting next to a cloud of smoke. A fat strand of red animal flesh hangs above the fire. She steps stiffly over to us, blowing the itching blackness from her nose.

"That's a good color on you," she smiles with yellowed teeth. Her broad face curls in concentration. "If only everyone knew back at the facility how easy it is to dye fabric! Then they would never get away with depriving color from half their people."

My eyes release their hold on the great, communal sun child. Now I study this woman's steep forehead. Her sheer presence is long, wise. Like she always holds her chin in the air.

"How did you..."

"My late husband came from the facility, too, but was exiled long before either of you were born. Neither of you would remember him. On the other hand, your f—"

"Would you mind telling her what you first told me? About how the world changed and about the facilities and everything?" Alden quickly interrupts, then licks his lips.

"Oh, you have to go back very, very far to understand. People were living in a way that polluted. And this pollution . . . well, it trapped the sun's heat, and made the world change. Perhaps the world would've changed anyway. Who knows. But storms quickly became stronger. The rain stopped falling. Glacial ice melted high in the mountains and never reformed. This took away the water that used to melt down to us in the spring. That's why the stream going into the lake dries up in the warm season. It needs rain to be full.

"Agriculture was a big thing back then. A handful of companies grew food for the whole world. The soil was already tired. So, when there was no more water, there was no more food, either. At this point, people panicked. They tried to take away the pollution, but it was too late. Even bigger glaciers at the corners of the Earth had melted. And they washed the oceans high onto the land.

"At this time there were millions, even billions, of people living in gigantic cities near the sea. They were forced to move inland, to squeeze in tighter. And, what with the lack of food and water and space, they started to spread disease.

"All those sick people crushed together, and they died off quick. Governments lost their control. Wars were fought over what was left. But not here. By then, half the world's population had died. Half the forests had been cut down. Half the animals were extinct. They always needed more and more resources. Because, to them, wealth didn't mean just providing for your family. It meant having more than everyone else.

"Water and air were dirty. But there were pockets . . . pockets of wilderness nearly pristine. So some of us came here to live with the earth. Where there were still animals to hunt and plants to forage. Others stayed in the cities. It's gotten better, but they'll never be what they once were.

"And then there were the facilities. Their creators began to build them long before the world changed. They knew it was coming. When my people came here, they ran after them, screaming that the sun was growing stronger. 'Come with us where it's safe,' they said, 'before it's too late. Only a few more years until the ozone layer is completely destroyed.' They tried to convince people that everyone would soon be forced to become nocturnal.

"The atmosphere has some holes in it, yes, that let the sun burn stronger. But since the pollution has gone away, we don't think it'll get any worse. That's what was causing it, after all. It might even get better. The air and water did. Some people, though, they got scared. The way everything had changed so fast . . . I can't blame them for being afraid it would get worse. So they went to live in the bubble.

"From there, you know what happened. How the story changed over generations. That the sun was already deadly. Had always been. That the outsiders were vicious killers. All concepts of self-reliance were lost. None of that was an accident. It was always part of the plan. To trick people into staying there and doing whatever the government says."

"But why would they do that?" I rub my hands together absently. Agitatedly. Picking away the dirt from under my fingernails. "Why would they trick all of us into hiding behind metal walls?"

"Because they wanted to keep living their lazy, selfish lifestyles. And you need other people for that," Berea's misty voice dies in a heavy stretch of wind.

Then I think of my mother. Of how she sits and waits in a cave of solitude, because she doesn't know what's outside of it. How ridiculous it is, to think of them all. How sad.

"How do you know all of this?" I whisper. What I really want to ask is how I can possibly trust her. But Alden does. Quickly, I glance at him. He slowly blinks his dark, black eyes. His ear-length hair falls in front of them.

"The facilities tell stories to gain control. We pass down our history so that our children can know what's happened, and make their own decisions accordingly," she stretches out her tan arms, gesturing to the sky. Now I notice that her ears are pierced with smooth black pins.

Alden and I move away from the fire, and from Berea. I don't know where we're going. It doesn't seem to matter. At least we won't be standing around, anymore, in the middle of things.

Even with all of this to think about, Alden makes me smile. He's alive, and I have him here. Now we can run together through the trees, beneath waving, drumming branches.

For the moment, we go nowhere. We walk in circles, talking. He looks at the falling sun and says, "It's getting late already."

Soon the village becomes crowded. By now I'm used to shirtless men, but not what they carry. One young man walks to the fire with a striped tail hanging over his arm. He sets down the dead animal. It wobbles on the grass, then jolts to solidity. Blood leaks out of its chest. Out of its pointy, open mouth.

Others cradle small carcasses. They cut open their kills, taking turns with a steel knife. It rips and tugs. The dirt is stained by spilling redness. By the severing of a body that is now just lumps of jiggling, textured food.

Some people sort through bright baskets of wild tendrils. The leaves flutter like quiet snakes. All these eyes, wide in concentration, dart up at me occasionally. Alden and I stand away, observing.

The animals are arranged on a rack above the enormous sun child. A woman with a necklace made of braided grass walks silently next to me.

"Hi Sempra. I'm Lake," she rests her delicate hand on my shoulder.

One by one they come to greet me. Wearing tattered sheets of cloth, or sturdy beige animal skins. Shoeless. The people next to me hold out their hands. Those across the fire-pit wave. I only nod my head, because they all know my name already. A few children run up to hug me. Laughing, I let their sticky hands encircle my legs.

There are too many names to remember. A round-faced woman with a pregnant stomach. One well-built man with only a square stub for a hand. Generations of families who all live in one house. Sometimes with two other families.

The old man who I first saw in the woods is called Tyler. His daughter is more beautiful than I thought possible. Her wavy hair sways at her waist, catching blonde wisps near her dark face.

"Reina," is all she says for an introduction. But her plump lips turn to Alden when she says it.

Dinner is shared on carved wooden trays. Silence is accompanied by whips of flame. I swallow a sweet cluster of leaves. Alden joins the others in consuming the leg of an animal. It leaves pink flakes in his teeth.

When we've finished, he grabs my arm tenderly away from the warmth. Together, we walk next to the lake. The cold air of night seems to fall from the stars. It's scooped up, washing over the water and around our skin. For a while we talk. About everything, about all.

"Look at the stars," I sing as we finally sit down on a long-dead tree. "I'll never get tired of them."

"Me neither."

I see the purple circles in his eyes, like the outline of a moonless night. He leans suddenly in. His thin mouth is gracefully aimed at mine. My hand creeps upward. It contorts into a dagger protecting my lips.

"What are you doing?" I push his surprised face away, my eyebrows knotted.

"I . . . I thought . . . because of what I . . . at the door when I left..." He swallows. "I thought you came . . . because you love me."

Across deserts and forests and hills and meadows I traveled to get to him. And never once did I ask myself this question. Never once did I think of Alden as more than my dearest friend. When we parted, we were still children, really. Here he is, tall. With muscles that pop from his arms. With strong cheekbones and a handsome, heavy face. But looking at him . . . he is still just a scrawny boy. He's still just . . . a friend.

"I wish I loved you, Alden." I say it with such a sadness that neither of us can doubt my sincerity. My stomach is heaved down by a new weight.

He stares at the night-bleached sand for a moment. Leans his elbows on his thighs.

"It's Timothy, isn't it?" He sighs. "You still love him."

"No! No, no, no. Alden, I left him behind. I left him behind four years ago. He was the one who got you kicked out! The whole thing . . . it was an act. The government hired him to get on my good side so he could find out where I got the book from. Because some guy across the street saw me and my mom with it that one day or night or I don't even know what to call it, when she was yelling at me," I let the words spill freely, out of breath. "Oh, Alden it's all my fault. I'm sorry. If it weren't for me—"

"If it weren't for you, we wouldn't be looking at the stars right now. Sempra, you're not here because you feel guilty, are you?" Alden stands up from the log. He speaks to the thousands of lights in the sky.

"No, of course not. There was nothing left for me there. Just a life without knowing. Just . . . I needed to see what was out here. If you were alive or not. You're my best friend, Alden. And a life in the facility didn't seem like much of a life at all. My only regret is not coming sooner."

"So you're over Timothy?"

"I never even loved him in the first place," I push myself up from the smooth wood.

Alden glances down at me.

"Okay. Just . . . Sempra? Let me know."

"Let you know what?" My voice rises.

"Let me know if you change your mind."

CHAPTER TWENTY-FOUR

Across the blue-dipped light, the forest's trees, I see a face. Not a face, really, but two eyes. Dancing. Gray and slanted, they pour silence into my mouth. They cough fire from the liquid that should be tears. I feel prickling nails of heat. Rimming this pair is a mask stitched from fur. The coarse hair of animal hide.

"Sempra," come whispers from limbless, decaying towers. "I know you as you shall be known. So listen..."

Then he's gone.

The red firelight, too, is gone. All I can see are tiny sun circles breaking through the entrance, through the smoke hole in the roof. Atop my thick bundle of blankets, I stretch. It smells like dirt, inside of here. Like the sunken place long hidden beneath a rock.

Voices drift around mutedly. I'm alone. Crawling out from under wool and fur, I change out of my facility clothes. Neatly, I fold them into a wooden storage box against the wall. After the streaks of mud were scrubbed away, I've used them as pajamas. By day, I wear orange that flows to my knees.

Beneath the sky, I smile at Berea. Her face seems less strong in the morning. Older. Using two sticks, she pulls a hot stone from the fire. With effortless balance, she drops it into a clay bowl. Inside float clouds of dark green.

"Mint tea?" I ask, lowering my nose closer.

"Good," she nods. "You've learned a lot in a week. When Alden first came he couldn't even tell the difference between mint and lavender!"

Down at the lake I splash water on my face. Knees pillowed by sparse grass. Eyes closed tight as cold, still water traces my cheek. A water bird spreads its black feathers. It floats quietly, stiffly turning its head. Two more join it, with matching white bands on their necks. They begin to shout. Talking to each other, I guess.

The village is almost empty already. Four women walk past me with furled clothes in their arms. They smile, young and ruddy. I stand watching from the shade of a tree. How they soak the clothes, then rub them with a foaming plant root. Scrub, rinse. Scrub, rinse. Twist until water leaks away. Then hang them over branches to dry.

"Water comes all the way up to these trees in the rainy season," Alden appears beside me. "See where the soil gets darker? That's how far it goes."

"It must rain a lot," I laugh. Because there's such a thing as rain.

"Some years," he shrugs.

My mind keeps moving. Each moment I think of my mother. And how I need to look for my father. And how amazing it is here, how similar it is to Mani's village. All these things rotate in some circle of thought.

"What is there to do around here?" I ask, still watching the clothes wrinkle in underwater shadows.

"Well, besides getting food, we gather firewood, and weave baskets, and carve wood. You know. Mend clothes, tan hides, or dry foods for the winter. Sometimes people try shaping clay or making weapons, but we usually just trade for those. Textiles, too. I guess some of the girls make jewelry..." Alden's gaze flies across the landscape. "How about we just go to the forest, for today?"

We run because we can. Because this is real, and beautiful. And we are here together. Alden lets his arms reach out. He grabs my open, flying hand. I don't mind. Leaping, we screech our joys across the open field.

Beneath our naked feet, spidery twigs crack. Our mouths hang open. On our faces are more than smiles. Dark, light, all shades of green shake over us in the forest's chill breath.

Carefully, we cut between dense thorn bushes. Wiry scratches streak our thighs, but our hands grip black berries. Purple juice dyes our tongues. First I suck away the sweetness, then chew the sour core. We eat until only one fat berry is left. That, we save for the birds.

"It's going to be hard to leave here," I sigh as we lay on our backs, every color of wildflower crowning our heads.

"What? No. No, you're not leaving." Dirt catches in Alden's hair.

"I have to, Alden. Maybe not now, but one of these days. I have to go look for my father. But then I'll come back again."

All that speaks is his moving chest. A fly lands on his short nose. He slaps it away, sitting up. When he does, a squirrel digs its fingers desperately into a tree trunk, climbing higher in a burst of motion. Yellow leaves float down to us. Alden stares at them, for a second. His black eyes lose any lightness. Closing them, with urgent creases along his brow, he parts his lips.

"Sempra. Your father's dead."

"I told you, he was really —"

"He lived here. In this village. I told them not to tell you. I told them I'd do it."

Slowly, steadily, he tells me.

When he first came into this world, how terrifying it was to be alone. When the sun rose for that first dawn, he ran. He hid all day in the same shack I did. Solitude beneath this great sky . . . it was too much. So Alden walked for days in the darkness. Searching for someone. Anyone. Even outsiders. The first ones he found were these people. Kind, though strange to him, they took him in.

The first time he mentioned me, a middle aged man came up to him. 'That's my daughter,' he said gruffly. This man knew my birth date, my mother's name. Everything.

"It seemed impossible. You always told me your father was dead. But it was obvious that he was telling the truth. That's why I stayed with them. I knew I had to hold on to him for you."

A sickness had overcome him long ago, when he first came to the outside. My father had been moving among villages. Deciding what to do, looking for his place. Figuring out how to get back to us. But the sickness left him blind. So, helpless, he stayed here.

"His eyes. They were this deep gray color. Sometimes it seemed like he could see more, not less. Your father was so calm. So wise. He taught me how to get by, out here. Every day we talked about going back to the facility. Going back to pull you out of there, if you never came yourself."

Alden would guide him through sight. My father would guide Alden through mind. Together they would rescue me, my mother, Alden's parents. Somehow, they'd send a message to us.

But then . . . but then my father was sick again. Something was wrong with his heart. He said he could feel it. Pale, hairless, panting with fatigue. For months and months, he grew weaker until . . .

"He was gone. They think he died in his sleep. I . . . I was the last one to talk to him, before . . . he told me to tell you that he loved you, even if he could never say it himself." Water lines Alden's eyes.

"How long ago did he die?" I choke.

"It doesn't really—"

"How long?" My jaw is tight.

Silence. Not even the wind dares speak.

"Four months ago."

Air is stolen from my throat. My eyes are too shocked, too still to cry.

I could have known my father if I had left three months earlier. If I hadn't waited for the cessation of fear. If I'd been brave enough to leave anytime in the last four, hideous, wasted years. What was I doing, sitting at a table, watching the TV wall? He could've been in my memory, too, not just Alden's. The man with the gray slanted eyes. I was too late. Too late. Too late. Forever, always, too late. And I will never, ever, in my entire life, see my own father's face.

Only in my dreams.

CHAPTER TWENTY-FIVE

Watch how the days move. Watch how they pile up and weigh down the sun. Horizon to horizon isn't quite as far, anymore. The god of all stars creeps low, coloring the world in faded flags of death. Deep reds saturate the leaves from within, wrinkling them to yellow and orange. Air swirls, and they are flown to the sodden soil. This ground is hidden by slick debris. By what will someday be new earth.

In the spring, they tell me, the trees will once again be clothed in fragile green flowers. But this is fall. Only the scaly limbs of the conifers remain green. Tall, so tall. These giants catch the wind and turn it in circles.

And so the rain is shed more often. The throaty calls of the Steller's jay fall silent. No more song sparrows whistle secret greetings to the sun. Gone too, is the smell that had long been coating the back of the air. Always strongest right before dusk. Some open, feral scent. It matched the steady glimmer beneath the sunset. I didn't know it changed with the seasons.

When the sky is white, a new coldness stands. Even during daylight. Soon we will have to wear fur, they say. And most animals will disappear. Just like the leaves, they'll vanish until spring. We store dried meat and plants in the wooden boxes. Buried underground, too. There will still be food to find, in the winter. But not a lot. Not enough.

There's less work to do in the garden. What remains after the harvest is left to return to the earth. Grass and leaves will decay into nutrients, nourishing the seeds they left as descendants.

Each morning Berea leads me through the forest. She points to a plant, and I tell her its name.

"Edible?" She questions, leaning against a tree with her arms crossed.

Most of them are, it turns out. We collect stems, dig up roots. All of it we arrange in uneven baskets that I wove myself.

Alden goes to hunt, instead. He carries a bow, rubs his skin with mud. All to shoot arrows into animal hearts. Reina follows closely behind to check the traps she set up in the days before. Sometimes her heavy stones have flattened squirrels or raccoons. I prefer not to see lifeless eyes.

But I have chewed dead flesh. Meat was the only thing to make my stomach full. So I thanked the animal. And I stole some of its life. When I rip roots from the ground, I say the same thing. That I'm sorry.

At night we sing the songs they brought with them from long ago. We connect pictures in the stars. Tyler, the old man I first met, holds his palms nightly to the heavens. Mars, he teaches me, is the reddest. Venus, the brightest. Lately, Jupiter has been nearly as vivid.

"All of those are planets. Other worlds entire!" He shouts to me, to all the children. "And around each of those little stars, there's millions more of them."

Everyone rests cross-legged on the ground. Alden sits closely with Reina. She laughs with her lip curled up, exposing remarkably white teeth. He strokes her shoulder with cupped fingers.

It didn't take me very long to realize how different Alden is. How he walks with his legs far apart, with comfort in his strong shoulders. How the first thing he does when he wakes up is stand under the sky with his eyes closed. Then he breathes in the wind. And he grins.

Of everyone, he's the most helpful. He goes around, asking if anyone needs anything done. Watching kids. Boiling water. Washing dishes. It's always on his mind that these people took him in.

"I owe them something," Alden tells me. "Even if it's just kindness."

I decided to try the same thing. Remembering what happened with Claire and Josh . . . I don't want to just be a guest again.

Through all this perfect happiness, my father and mother weigh on me. My chin dips down. After smiling, my lips quickly fall flat again. The man with the gray slanted eyes has been absent from my dreams. He's the one who led me here, I know it.

My father is dead, but my mom is still alive. To think of her worn face, all alone in front of the TV wall . . . she's not going to know. She'll never know what the outside is really like unless someone tells her. I can't let her die like that. Without ever running on grass. Or counting the moon's many shapes. Or feeling raindrops on her skin.

She can't die until I see her again.

So my plan is to travel back to the facility. Before this horrible thing called winter comes. Maybe there's nothing I can do, but I have to try. Then we will come back and live here. With Alden.

Alden, who cuts the rabbit he killed today into slices. The first plate, he hands to Reina. She tears off a strip with her hands, nibbling the golden meat. I receive the next wooden square. And a much smaller piece. Gently, I let the flavor soak into my tongue.

Food here, everything, has smell and flavor. It's almost hard to remember what mush tasted like. Or if it even tasted like anything at all.

When we're in the hut, with only shadows of fire on the walls, I turn to Alden. He's half asleep on the blankets next to mine. All I can see is his hair spilling over.

"Alden. I have to tell you something."

A man grumbles a snore from across the room. The air is heavy. Alden scoots up, faces me.

"I'm leaving tomorrow morning," I whisper hoarsely. "I'm going back to the facility to look for my mom. There's probably no way in, but I have to try it. She needs to . . . she needs to know. Don't worry, though. I'll come back. I should be back in about two weeks. Tell the others tomorrow, okay?"

For a moment I don't think he heard me. All he does is stare, but he has no eyes. Then he crouches up from his bed. Without taking a breath, he drops to his knees on the dirt floor. Leaning over me. I prop myself on my elbow. He takes my chin in his warm hand, and kisses my cheek. Softly. With such care that I want him to kiss my lips, too.

No words. He slips soundlessly into his blankets.

I can't let my eyelids close. There's something in my chest, something I've never felt before. But it fast dissolves. Because, with hatred, I think of Reina.

CHAPTER TWENTY-SIX

Morning falls lightly on my lap. I wake before the sun does. In a woven satchel I carry dried food, water, a rolled up blanket, flint. With this strung across my chest, I step blindly over the sleeping bodies.

Without sunlight, the world is wet with dew. Opposite the distant hills, an edge of the sky begins to fade to soft blue. It will be warm today, I can already tell. There is a transparency to the low clouds stifling the stars.

Before the forest takes it away, I look back at the village. The last traces of smoke empty from the hut roofs. There is a stillness interrupted only by robin songs. And by Alden, jogging over to me with a red face.

"What are you doing here?" I hiss, because yelling wouldn't fit the blending, unawake colors. "You don't have to come."

"But I do," his heavy breath clouds into fog. "The way I came is twice as fast as going up through the hills. Besides, I have this."

He reaches into his own bag, made of crude beige fabric. What he pulls out is a thin paper book. On its cover, an animal with its snout raised high. A wolf.

"How . . . I thought they took that away from you?" I reach out for it, and rub the pages between my fingers. The musty smell drifts to my nose.

"I stuck it in my pocket right before they kicked me out. They must've seen me, but they didn't say anything. I guess they didn't care, as long as it was gone. Anyway, I have an idea."

We scrape shriveled blackberries into a pile, and crush them beneath a stone. Their blood becomes ink. With a pointed stick, we write on the inside cover. It's hard to shape the letters with our own hands. Alden manages a shaky message. *The sun will not kill you. The outsiders are not evil. They lied to you. Come outside. We are Alden and Sempra, and we are still alive.*

If we can't get to my mom, maybe *The Call of the Wild* can.

"We did it. We answered the call," I laugh as we walk beneath the trees. Then a sigh escapes my lips. Before I've even let myself consider it, I say, "I think my wish came true."

Alden glances at me, his wide cheeks rising.

"You mean—"

"I love you, Alden. I love you more than the sun, and the moon, and all the stars in the sky." He knows how much I love these things. They make the world whole, and burn the sky with fire.

The moment I realize we've stopped walking is the moment he kisses me. Lips on lips. His arms wrap around my waist.

"What about Reina? Don't you still love her?" I pull timidly away, squinting up at him.

"Sempra, I never loved her at all."

Suddenly, then, the sun bares his face to the mountains. All of Earth is reflected in the currents of the air. In the soaring tides of a place where everything is alive. I feel it. The spirit in the eyes. This energy that is life, the glow of connection. In the crow that chases smaller birds. In the stream that flows downhill. In the flower, wilted after a storm, with holes chewed in it by caterpillars.

Those people who only wanted things, and money, and land. Who spilt the carcasses of ancient forestlands. Who poisoned their own mouths. They forgot how to see. They took too much, until there was nothing left. And now, in the end we have returned to the beginning. To the ways all people lived before the forgetfulness. Once again we are wild creatures. Wolves.

Alden and I travel for three days. We stop to eat bedstraw, wild carrots, a few sour huckleberries. In near darkness, I make a spark with flint. Alden aims his bow at the yellow eyes of an opossum. I look away.

One night I dream of sheets, of linens. They're dotted with gray eyes drawn in slanted berry ink.

Finally, the facility shines in the dimming light. Meadow grass blows away, into dusty desert sand. We make our way, never growing closer. Rusty flowers curve on crooked stems. My sight adjusts to the lack of color. My ears, to the winded silence.

At the edge of our previous world we stand. Sunset glares off of its black solar panels.

"Now what?" He asks.

"I guess we should just walk around the whole thing. Follow the perimeter. Maybe there really is a window."

So we pull along our tired legs. Around and around until the sun is on its way again. An edge of the wall seems to sway. It ripples in the wind. Looking closer, I see it's made of fabric. A square hole covered by a worn gray cloth.

Desperately, I burst my groping fingers through. Lift up the tattered rag. There sits a young man. Seeing my face, he leaps up from his metal chair. His round eyes grow, his mouth opens.

"Who are you?"

"What," Alden already has the book out, "you've never seen an outsider before?"

"I only look out there, just . . . sometimes. My grandfather showed it to me. No . . . no one ever looks in," the man trembles.

I tell the man my mother's name, where she lives, and beg him to take the book to her.

"After she sees it, you might want to read it yourself," I smile.

Six Months Later

I hand my mother a plate of dandelion greens, of pink fireweed. She lets her teeth glow in the sunlight.

She came with us, slowly unlearning her fears. My grandmother stayed. So did Alden's parents, though my mom tried to convince all of them.

We sit next to the fire. Berea and my mother are good friends. They spent the morning throwing water on the garden. Our lives here are simple, vivid. My mother's embrace holds no tiredness.

When I told her about my father, she wasn't surprised.

"I always had a feeling that he was gone," she nearly mouthed, voiceless.

Alden comes from behind, kissing my forehead.

"I don't think I'll ever get used to the way the fire moves," my mom watches the dancing heat.

"You know," I laugh, "when I first came here, I thought the fire looked like the sun's child. I still call it sun child in my head."

Alden stares at me.

"Sempra, that's what your father called us. The people who live out here. He used to call us sun children."

Startled, I take a deep breath. It smells like smoke. Like black clouds and the coming of summer.

"He's right. Everything starts with the sun." I look at the sky. At the flickering cottonwood trees in the wind. Then at the fire itself. "We are sun children."

ACKNOWLEDGMENTS

I'd like to acknowledge everyone who has supported me: my parents, Francisco and Traci, and my brother, Nico; Grandma Pat, Aunt Amy, Uncle Danny, Jacob, Aunt Shirley, Uncle Donny, Uncle Dale, Lulu, Tía Lita, Tío Alex, Vanessa, Alexandra, and Barbara; all of my friends, especially Jenna, Tess, Amy, and Arlene; and my dog, Ginger.

HOMEBOUND PUBLICATIONS

Ensuring that the mainstream isn't the only stream.

At Homebound Publications, we publish books written by independent voices for independent minds. Our books focus on a return to simplicity and balance, connection to the earth and each other, and the search for meaning and authenticity. Founded in 2011, Homebound Publications is one of the rising independent publishers in the country. Collectively through our imprints, we publish between fifteen to twenty offerings each year. Our authors have received dozens of awards, including: *Foreword Reviews'* Book of the Year, Nautilus Book Award, Benjamin Franklin Book Awards, and Saltire Literary Awards. Highly-respected among bookstores, readers and authors alike, Homebound Publications has a proven devotion to quality, originality and integrity.

We are a small press with big ideas. As an independent publisher we strive to ensure that the mainstream is not the only stream. It is our intention at Homebound Publications to preserve contemplative storytelling. We publish full-length introspective works of creative non-fiction as well as essay collections, travel writing, poetry, and novels. In all our titles, our intention is to introduce new perspectives that will directly aid humankind in the trials we face at present as a global village.

WWW.HOMEBOUNDPUBLICATIONS.COM